"Who'd have guessed it?"

Nina cuddled closer to John as she spoke. A smile softened her lips.

"Guessed what?" John looked into her eyes, and his brow creased in a frown that was here and gone.

"That slow, thoughtful John Sawyer was a crackerjack of unleashed virility in bed."

John's cheeks were already flushed, but Nina could have sworn that they grew more so. "I was inspired," he murmured.

"You certainly were." Her smile faded. She touched his face. "I didn't like you much when we first met. You were slowing me down."

"I still am. It's my cause."

"It won't work. I have to be at the office by 10:00 a.m. . . . unless you can convince me otherwise."

John kissed her gently, then less gently as his hunger grew. He rolled onto his back and pulled Nina on top of him. "Mmm . . ." Nina whispered. "Convince me more. . . ."

Dear Reader,

Welcome to Crosslyn Rise, a majestic estate on the North Shore of Massachusetts and the setting for Barbara Delinsky's long-awaited trilogy; three love stories that stand alone but together create a powerful saga of six lives linked by a common dream. The Crosslyn Rise trilogy appears in three consecutive months, beginning in October with *The Dream* and followed in November and December with *The Dream Unfolds* and *The Dream Comes True*.

Harlequin Temptation is proud to feature these dynamic, passionate romances from one of our finest authors, and we'd love to hear your comments. Please take the time to write to us.

The Editors
Harlequin Temptation
225 Duncan Mill Road
Don Mills, Ontario, Canada
M3B 3K9

CROSSLYN RISE

The Dream Comes True
BARBARA DELINSKY

Harlequin Books

TORONTO • NEW YORK • LONDON
AMSTERDAM • PARIS • SYDNEY • HAMBURG
STOCKHOLM • ATHENS • TOKYO • MILAN

Published December 1990

ISBN 0-373-25425-3

CROSSLYN RISE: THE DREAM COMES TRUE

1

EIGHT PEOPLE SAT around the large table in the boardroom at Gordon Hale's bank. They comprised the Crosslyn Rise consortium, the men and women who were financing the conversion of Crosslyn Rise from an elegant, singly owned estate to an exclusive condominium community. Of the eight, seven seemed perfectly content with the way the early-morning meeting was going. Only Nina Stone was frustrated.

Nina hated meetings, particularly the kind where people sat at large tables and hashed things out ad nauseam. Discussion was part of the democratic process, she knew, and as a member of the consortium, with a goodly portion of her own savings at stake, she appreciated having a say in what was happening at Crosslyn Rise. So she had smilingly endured all of the meetings that had come in the months before. But this one was different. This discussion was right up her alley. She was the expert here. If her fellow investors weren't willing to take her professional advice now that the time had finally come for her to give it, she didn't know why in the world she was wasting her time.

Nina's business was real estate. She was the broker of record for Crosslyn Rise, the one who would be in charge of selling the units and finding tenants for the retail space. It was mid-May, nearly eight months since ground had been broken, and the project was finally ready to be marketed.

"I still think," she said for the third time in thirty minutes, "that pricing in the mid-fives is shooting low. Given location alone, we can ask six or seven. What other complex is forty minutes from Boston, tucked into trees and meadows, and opening onto the ocean? What other complex offers a health club, a catering service, meeting rooms and even guest rooms to rent out for visiting friends and relatives? What other complex offers both a marina and shops?"

"None," Carter Malloy conceded, "at least, not in this area." Carter was the architect for the project and the unofficial leader of the consortium. As of the previous fall, he was married to Jessica Crosslyn, who sat close by his side. Jessica's family had been the original owners of the Rise. "But the real estate market is lousy. The last thing we want is to overprice the units, then have them sit empty for years."

"They won't sit empty," Nina insisted. "Trust me. I know the market. They'll sell."

Jessica wasn't convinced. "Didn't you tell me that things weren't selling in the upper end of the market?"

"Uh-huh, but that was well over a year ago, when you were thinking of selling the Rise intact, to a single buyer. Selling something in the multiple millions was tough then. It's eased up, even more so in the range we're talking." She sent her most confident glance around the table. "As your broker, I'd recommend pricing from high sixes to mid sevens, depending on the size of the unit. Based on other sales I've made in the past few months, I'm sure we can get it."

"What kind of sales were those?" came the quiet voice of John Sawyer from the opposite end of the table.

Nina homed in on him as she'd been doing, it seemed, for a good part of the past hour. Of all those in the room, he disturbed her the most, and it wasn't his overgrown-schoolboy look—round wire-rimmed glasses, slightly shaggy brown hair, corduroy blazer with elbow patches and open-necked plaid shirt—that did it. It was the fact that he was sticking his nose in where it didn't belong. He was a bookseller, not a businessman. He knew nothing about real estate, and though she had to admit that he usually stayed in the background, he wasn't staying in the background today. In his annoyingly laid-back and contemplative way, he was questioning nearly everything she said.

"Three of those sales were in the eights, one in the nines, and another well over the million mark," she told him.

"For properties like ours?" he challenged softly.

She didn't blink. "No. The properties were very different, but the point is that, A, this community is in demand, and, B, there is money around to be spent."

"But by what kinds of people?" he countered in the slow way he had of speaking. "Of course, the super-wealthy can spend it, but the superwealthy aren't the ones who'll be moving here. They won't want condo living when they can have ten-acre estates of their own. I thought we were aiming at the middle-aged adult whose children are newly grown and out of the house and who now wants something less demanding. That kind of person doesn't have seven or eight hundred thousand dollars to toss around. He's still feeling his way out from under college tuitions."

"That's one way of looking at it," Nina acknowledged. "Another way is that he now has money to spend that he hasn't had before, precisely because he no longer has those tuitions to shoulder. And he'll be willing to spend it. As he sees it, he's sacrificed a whole lot to raise his family. Now he's ready to do things for himself. That's why the concept of Crosslyn Rise is so perfect. It appeals to the person who is still totally functional, the person who is at the height of his career and isn't about to wait for retirement to pamper himself. He has the money. He'll spend it."

"What about the shopkeepers?" John asked.

"What about them?"

"They don't have it to spend. If you set the price of the condos so high, the rental space will have to be accordingly high, which will rule out the majority of the local merchants."

"Not necessarily."

"You'll give them special deals?"

"The rental space doesn't have to be that high."

"It can't be anywhere *near* that high—"

Her eyes flashed. "Or you won't move in?"

"I won't be *able* to move in," he said calmly.

With a glance at his watch, Gideon Lowe, the builder for the project, suddenly sat forward. "I don't know about you guys, but it's already nine. I'm losin' the best part of my day." He slanted a grin from Nina to John. "How about you two stay on here and bicker for a while, then give us a report on what you decide at the meeting next week?"

Nina didn't appreciate the suggestion, particularly since she suspected that Gideon's rush was more to see his wife than his men. She couldn't blame him, she supposed; he'd been married less than a month and was clearly in love. His wife, Christine, was doing the decorating for Crosslyn Rise. Nina liked her a lot.

Still, this was business. Nina didn't like the idea of staying on to bicker with John Sawyer when she wanted an immediate decision from the group. Keeping her voice as pleasant as possible, given the frustration she was feeling, she said, "I think this is something for the committee as a whole to decide. Mr. Sawyer is only one man—"

"One man," Carter interrupted, "who is probably in a better position than any of the rest of us to discuss the money issues you're talking about. He's our potential shopkeeper."

Jessica agreed. "Maybe Gideon is right. If the two of you toss ideas back and forth and come up with some kind of compromise before next week, you'll save us all some time. We're running a little short now. Carter has an appointment at nine-thirty in Boston, I have one in Cambridge." Murmurs of agreement came from around the table, along with the scuffing of chair legs on the highly polished oak floor.

"But I wanted to go to the printer with the brochure," Nina said, barely curbing her impatience as she stood along with the others. "I need the price information for that."

Carter snapped his briefcase shut. "We'll make the final decision next week." To John, he said, "You'll meet with Nina?"

Nina looked at John. The fact that he was still seated didn't surprise her at all. The consortium had met no less than a dozen times since its formation, and in all that time, not once had she seen him in a rush. He spoke slowly. He moved slowly. If she didn't know better, she'd have thought that he didn't have a thing in life to do but mosey along when the mood hit and water the geraniums in the window box outside the small Victorian that housed his bookstore.

But she did know better. She knew that John Sawyer ran that bookstore with the help of only one other person, a middle-aged woman named Minna Larken, who manned the till during the hours when John was with his son. Nina also knew that the boy was four, that he had severe sight and hearing problems and that her heart went out to both father and son. But that didn't make her any less impatient. She had work to do, a name to build and money to make, and John Sawyer's slow and easygoing manner made her itchy.

Typically, in response to Carter's query, John was a minute in answering. Finally he said, "I think we could find a time to meet."

Forcing a smile, Nina ruffled the back of her dark boy-short hair and said in a way that she hoped sounded sweet but apologetic, "Wow, this week is a tough one. I have showings one after another today and tomorrow, then a seminar Thursday through Sunday."

"That leaves Monday," Carter said buoyantly. "Monday's perfect." Putting an arm around Jessica's waist, he ushered her from the room.

"Carter?" Nina called, but he didn't answer. "Jessica?"

"I'll talk with you later," Jessica called over her shoulder, then was gone, as were all of the others except John. Feeling thwarted, Nina sent him a helpless look.

With measured movements, he sat back in his chair. "If it's any consolation, I don't like the idea of this any more than you do."

She didn't know whether to be insulted. "Why not?"

"Because you're always in a rush. You make me nervous."

She *was* insulted, which was why she set aside her normal tact and said, "Then we're even, because you're so slow, you make *me* nervous." But it looked as though the group would be expecting some sort of decision from John and her, and she couldn't afford to let them down. There were some important people among them. Impressing important people was one way to guarantee future work.

Hiking her bag from the floor to the table, she fished out her appointment book. "So, when will it be? Do you want to make it sometime next Monday, say late morning?"

John laced his fingers before him. "Next Monday is bad for me. I'll be in Boston all day."

"Okay." She flipped back a page, then several more. The seminar would be morning to night, and draining. No way could she handle a meeting with John on any of those days. "I could squeeze something in between three-thirty and four tomorrow afternoon."

He considered that, then shook his head. "I work then."

"So do I," she said quickly, "but the point is to fudge a little here and there." She ran a glossy fingernail down the page. "My last showing is at seven, but then I have a meeting—" She cut herself off, mumbled, "Forget that," and turned back one more page. "How about later today?"

When he didn't answer, she looked up. Only then did he ask, "How much later?"

She studied her book. "I have appointments through seven. We could meet after that."

He freed one of his hands to rub the side of his nose, under his glasses. When the glasses had stopped bobbing and his fingers were laced again, he said, "No good. I'm with my son then."

"What time does he go to bed?"

"Seven-thirty, eight."

"We could meet then. Can you get a sitter?"

"I can, but I won't. I have work to do in the store."

"But if you don't have a sitter—"

"I live on the second floor of the house. If I'm downstairs in the store and he cries, I can hear it."

She sighed. "Okay. What time will you finish your work?" It occurred to her that she would rather meet with John later that day, even if it meant cutting into the precious little time she had to herself, than having the meeting hanging over her head all week.

"Nine or ten."

"We could meet then. I'll come over."

He eyed her warily. "Isn't that a little late for a meeting?"

"Not if there's no other time, and it looks like there isn't."

His wariness persisted. "Don't you ever stop?"

"Sure. When I go to bed, which is usually sometime around one or two in the morning. So—" she wanted to get it settled and leave "—are we on for nine, or would you rather make it ten?"

"And you work all day long?"

"Seven days a week," she said with pride, because pride was what she felt. Of six brokers in her office, her sales figures had been the highest for three years running. Granted, she didn't have a husband or children to slow her down, but the fact remained that she worked hard.

"When do you relax?"

"I don't need to relax."

"Everyone needs to relax."

"Not me. I get pleasure in working." She held her pen poised over the appointment book. "Nine, or ten?"

He studied her in silence for a minute. "Nine. Any later and I won't be thinking straight. Unlike you, I'm human."

His voice was as unruffled as ever. She searched his face for derision, but given the distance down the table and the fact of the glasses shielding his eyes, she came up short. "I'm human," she said quietly, if a bit defensively. "I just like to make the most of every minute." By way of punctuation, she snapped the appointment book shut, returned it to her bag and hung the bag on her shoulder. "I'll see you at nine," she said on her way out the door.

There was no sound behind her, but then, she hadn't expected there would be. John Sawyer would have needed at least thirty seconds to muster a response, but she'd been gone in fifteen. By the time the next fifteen had passed, her thoughts were three miles down the road in her office.

WITHIN FIFTEEN MINUTES, after stops at the post office and the dry cleaner, she was there herself. Crown Realty occupied the bottom floor of a small office building on the edge of town. The brainchild of Martin Crown, the firm was an independent one. It had the advantage over some of the larger franchises in its ties to the community; the Crown family had been on the North Shore for generations. Over and above two local restaurants and a shopping mall, the family assets included the weekly newspaper that made its way as far as Boston. In that weekly newspaper were real estate ads that would have cost an arm and a leg elsewhere. The money saved was tallied into profits, and profits were what interested Nina Stone the most.

Nina had plans for the future. She was going to have her own firm, have her own staff, have money in the bank, stability and security. She'd known this for ten years, the first four of which she'd spent in New York. Four years had taught her that as tough as she was, New York was tougher. So she'd moved to the North Shore of Massachusetts, where the living was easier and the market was hot. For six years, she'd doggedly worked her way up in the world of real estate. Now the end was in sight. With one more year like the ones behind her and a respectable return on her investment in Crosslyn Rise, she'd have enough money to go out on her own.

Having a solid name, a successful business and scads of money meant independence, and independence meant the world to Nina.

"Hi, Chrissie," she called with a smile as she strode through the reception area. "Any calls?"

"Pink slips are on your desk," was the receptionist's reply.

Depositing her bag, Nina snatched them up, glanced through even as she rearranged them in order of importance, then settled into her chair and reached for the phone. The first and most urgent call was from a lawyer whose client was to pass papers on a piece of property that morning. At his request, the meeting was put off for an hour, which meant that Nina had to shift two other appointments. Then she returned calls to a seller with a decision on pricing, an accountant trying to negotiate his way into prime business space and a potential buyer who had heard a rumor that the price of the house she was waiting for was about to drop.

Nina was on the phone chasing down that rumor when a young woman appeared at her door. Lee Stockland, with her frizzy brown hair, her conservative skirts, blouses and single strand of pearls, and the ten extra pounds she'd been trying to lose forever, was a colleague. She was also a good friend, one of the best Nina had. Their personalities complemented each other.

Nina waved her in, then held up a finger and spoke into the phone.

"Charlie Dunn, please."

"I'm sorry, Mr. Dunn's not in the office."

"This is Nina Stone at Crown Realty. It's urgent that I speak with him." She glanced at her watch. "I'll be here for another forty-five minutes. If he comes in during that time, would you have him call me?"

"Certainly."

"Thanks." She hung up and turned to Lee. "Maisie Stewart heard that 23 Hammond dropped to eight-fifty." She swiveled in her chair. "It wasn't in the computer last night. Have you seen anything today?"

"Nope."

Nina brought up the proper screen, punched in the listing she wanted and saw that Lee was right. She sat back in her chair. "If word of mouth beat this computer, I'll be furious. Charlie knows the rules. Any change is supposed to be entered here."

"Charlie isn't exactly a computer person."

Nina tossed a glance skyward. "Do tell. He claims you can't teach an old dog new tricks, but I don't agree with that for a minute. What you make up your mind to do, you do." With barely a breath, she said, "So, what did the Millers think of the house?"

Lee took the chair by Nina's desk. "They weren't thrilled to see me rather than you, but I think they liked it. Especially her, and that's what counts."

Nina nodded. "I know him. He'll see every little flaw and be tallying up how much it will cost to fix each one. Then he'll balance the amount against the price of the house and go back and forth, back and forth until someone else's bid is accepted and it's too late. Then we'll start right back at the beginning again." She sighed, suddenly sheepish, and fiddled with her earring. "Thanks, Lee. Jason is a pain in the butt. I really appreciate your taking them out."

"You appreciate it?" Lee laughed. "I'm the one who appreciates it. If it weren't for the clients you give me, I'd be twiddling my thumbs all day."

Nina couldn't argue with that. As brokers went, Lee was an able technician. Given a client, she did fine. But she didn't know the meaning of the word 'hustle,' and hustling was the name of the game. Nina hustled. When she wasn't showing a potential buyer a piece of property, she was meeting with a seller, or phoning potential others with offers of appraisals, or organizing mailings to keep her name and her business in the forefront of the community's mind.

Lee didn't have the drive for that, and while once upon a time Nina had scolded her friend, she didn't any longer. Lee was perfectly happy to work less, to earn less, in essence to serve as Nina's assistant, and Nina was grateful for the help. "You're a lifesaver," she said. "The Millers insisted on going early this morning. I couldn't be two places at once."

"Speaking of which," she gave a pointed look at Nina's bright red linen dress, "I take it that's your power outfit. How did it go at the bank?"

Nina's mouth drew down at the corners. "Don't ask."

"Not good?"

"Slow. Sl-ow." She began to pull folders from her bag. "Let me tell you, working with so many people is a real hassle. To get one decision made is a major ordeal."

"Did they like the brochure?"

"I think so, but I never got a final judgment on it, because they got hung up discussing the pricing of the units."

"What did they decide on that?"

Nina's phone buzzed. *"Nothing,"* she cried, letting her frustration show. "They want me to meet with this one guy—" She picked up the phone. "Nina Stone."

"Ms. Stone, my name is Carl Anderson. I was given your name by Peter Serretti, who worked with you on your new computer system."

Nina remembered Peter clearly. He had indeed worked with her, far more closely than she had wanted. Long after she learned to operate the system, she'd been plagued by phone calls from Peter asking her out. So now his friend was calling. She was immediately on her guard.

"Of course, I remember Mr. Serretti. What can I do for you, Mr. Anderson?"

"I'm actually calling from New York. My wife and I are both in education. We'll be moving to Boston in August. We were thinking of buying something on the North Shore. Pete said you were the one to talk with."

Nina felt an immediate lightening of her mood. "I'm sure I am," she said with a smile for Lee, who had settled into her chair to wait. "What kind of place are you looking for?"

"A condo. Two to three bedrooms. We have no children, but have a dog and two cars."

Nina was making notes. "Price range?"

"Two-fifty, three hundred tops." He rushed on apologetically. "We just can't handle anything more than that. When we visited Pete, we were impressed with the North Shore. If I'm totally out of my league, tell me."

"You're not, not at all." Crosslyn Rise was out of the question, both in terms of price and availability, but there were other options. "There's an older three-bedroom condo on the market for two-ninety-five, and several more updated two-bedrooms in the same range. But there's a new complex that you should probably see. It's in Salem, near the harbor, and it's beautiful. About half of the units have been sold, but there are still some wonderful three-bedroom ones that would fall within your range." She described the units, at times reading directly from the promotional packet that Lee had smoothly slipped her.

Carl seemed pleased. "We thought we'd drive up Friday and spend Saturday and Sunday looking. Would that be all right?"

"Uh, unfortunately, I'll be at a seminar all weekend—" her eyes met Lee's "—but one of my associates could certainly show you as much as you'd like to see." She frowned when, with a helpless look, Lee gave a quick shake of her head.

"Pete recommended you," Carl insisted. "He said you knew what you were talking about. I had an awful time with a broker here when we bought the place we're in now. She messed up the Purchase and Sales agreement, and we nearly lost the place."

Nina loved hearing stories like that. "I don't mess up Purchase and Sales agreements."

"That's what Pete said."

"Is this weekend the only time you can come?"

"This is the only weekend my wife and I are both free."

"Then let me suggest this. I'll go through all the listings, come up with everything I think might be worth seeing, and my associate will do the showing." Lee was still looking helpless. "You and I can talk first thing Monday morning when I'm back in the office. I'll be able to handle things from there."

Carl Anderson seemed satisfied with that. After taking note of his address and phone number, plus additional information regarding what he wanted, Nina hung up the phone. Her eyes quickly met Lee's. "Problem?"

"I can't work this weekend," Lee said timidly.

"Oh, Lee. You said you could. I've been counting on you to cover for me while I'm away."

"I can for Thursday and Friday, but—" she hesitated for a split second before blurting out "—Tom wants to go to the Vineyard. I've never been to the Vineyard. He's already made reservations for the ferry and the hotel, and he's talking about lying on the beach and browsing through the shops and eating at terrific restaurants—" She caught her breath and let out a soft, "How could I say no?"

Nina felt a surge of frustration that had nothing to do with work. "You can't. You never can, to Tom. But it's always last minute to a dinner or a movie or a weekend away. Why doesn't he call sooner?"

"He just doesn't plan his life that way. He likes spontaneity."

"Baloney. He just can't make any kind of commitment. He goes here, goes there, calls you when he gets the urge. He uses you, Lee."

"But I like him."

"You're too good for him."

"I'm not," Lee said flatly. "I'm twenty-eight, and I've never been married. I'm not cute like you, or petite, or blue eyed. I can't wear clothes like you do or polish my nails like you do. I'm not aggressive, and I'll never earn much money, so I'm not much of a bargain. But Tom is good to me."

Nina died a little inside. Each time she heard a woman use those words, no matter how innocent they were, she thought of her mother. So many times Maria Stone had said the same—*but he's good to me*—and for all the men who'd been "good" to her, she had ended up with nothing. Nina ached at the thought of that happening again, particularly to someone she cared about, like Lee.

Coming forward on the desk, she said with force, "You're not a lost cause, Lee. You're attractive and smart and warm. You're the one who taught me how to cook, and arrange flowers, and save bundles by shopping in the stores *you* found. You have lots to offer a man, lots more than me. You don't need to stoop to the level of a Tom Brody. If you want male company, there are plenty of other men around."

"Fine for you to say. You attract them like flies, then you swat them away."

"I do not."

"You're not interested in a relationship."

"I'm not interested in marriage, and I'm not interested in being kept, but I date. If an interesting guy comes along and asks me to dinner, I go."

"When you have time."

"Is there anything wrong with that?" Nina asked more gently. They'd had the discussion before. "Work means a lot to me. It's my future. At this point in my life, the investment I make in it means a whole lot more than the investment I might make in a man." Under her breath, she muttered, "Heaven only knows the return stands to be better."

Lee heard the low muttering and sighed. "Speak for yourself. Those of us who aren't so independent are looking all over for Mr. Right, but I think all the Mr. Rights are taken."

"Just wait. Give all those Mr. Rights a chance to divorce their first wives, then they'll be yours for the taking. I'm told they're far better husbands the second time around."

"I want Tom first. I think I have a chance with him, Nina. I really do."

But Nina knew more about Tom Brody than she let on. She had seen him in action against her boss years before, when he'd tried to renege on an agreement that was signed and sealed. "He's not right for you, Lee. He's a huckster with his eye out for the fast lane. When he hooks onto it, he'll be long gone. What you need is someone softer, slower, less driven." The image that popped unbidden into her mind made her snort. "You need a guy like John Sawyer."

"Who's John Sawyer?"

"A member of my consortium. He's invested in the Rise, but he's not a businessman, at least, not in the strictest sense of the word. He sells books. He's a thinker."

Lee arched an interested brow. "Married?"

"His wife died. He has a little boy who's four."

Lee's interest waned. "Oh. I'm no good with kids. I don't think I want to get into that. Forget John Sawyer."

Nina's thoughts flipped back to the meeting earlier that morning, then ahead to the one to come later that night. "I wish I could. The man might prove to be the biggest thorn in my side since Throckmorton Malone." Throckmorton Malone was a perennial house-shopper. He found a house he liked, put down a deposit, started bickering with either the builder or the owner or the owner's agent about the smallest, most insignificant details, then pulled out of the deal after handfuls of others who might have been interested had been turned away.

"No one could be that big a thorn."

Nina sighed. "Maybe. Still, this one could give me gray hair. He thinks we're pricing the units too high. He thinks he knows the market. Worst of all, the rest of the group thinks he knows what he's talking about, so they're making me meet separately with him to try to come to some sort of compromise."

"That's not so bad. You can convince him to see things your way."

"Yeah, but he's so—" she made a face as she searched for the word, finally exploding into a scornful "—*blah*. He's so calm and casual and unhurried about everything. He has all the time in the world to mull over every little thing. What ought to take five minutes will take fifty with him. Just looking at him frustrates me."

Lee showed a hint of renewed interest. "He's good-looking?"

"Not to *my* way of thinking. He's too bookish. I mean, we're talking thin and pale. Drab. Boring."

"Is he tall?"

Nina had to think about that, then think some more. "I don't know. I don't think so. Funny, I've never really noticed. He's that kind of guy, blink and you miss him." She frowned. "Mostly when I see him he's sitting down. Everyone else get up to leave, he stays in his seat. He doesn't move quickly. Ever." She sighed. "And I have to meet with him at nine o'clock tonight. Who knows how long he'll drag out the meeting." She grimaced. "Could be he'll put me to sleep."

"That'd be novel." They both knew Nina rarely slept. She had too much energy to slow down for long.

With a glance at her watch, Nina was out of her chair. "I'm meeting with the Selwyns at the Traynor cape in five minutes. Gotta run."

"About this weekend—" Lee began.

"Not to worry," Nina assured her. Taking a file from the corner of the desk, she slipped it into her bag. "I'll get someone else to cover."

"I'm really sorry. I hate letting you down."

Turning to her, Nina said in earnest, "You're not letting me down, at least not about filling in here. You have a right to a life, and if you haven't been to the Vineyard, you *have* to go. I just wish you weren't going with Tom."

"I'll be fine. Really."

"Famous last words," Nina said softly, gave Lee a last pleading look, then murmured, "Gotta run."

2

NINA'S DAY WAS BUSY ENOUGH to prevent her from giving the impending meeting with John much thought until she returned to her office at seven, with all other appointments behind her and two hours to fill before nine. Filling them wasn't the problem. She had more than enough paperwork to do, and if she finished that, there were phone calls to make. But the urgency wasn't the same as it would have been at the height of the workday. So her mind wandered.

She thought about Crosslyn Rise, and how pretty the first of the units, nestled in among trees at the duck pond, were beginning to look. She thought about the brochure she had so painstakingly put together with the artist who'd drawn pictures of the Rise, and the printer, and the fact that she felt it should already be in circulation. She thought about the pricing, the arguments both ways, her own conviction and John's. She thought about his slow, slow way of thinking and talking and her own preference for working more quickly. The more she thought about those things, the more frustrated she grew. By the time she finally got into her car and drove to The Leaf Turner, she was spoiling for a fight.

The house stood close to the center of town and was a small white Victorian, set in relief against the night by the glow of a street lamp that stood nearby. The second floor was dark, the first floor lit. Walking to the front door as though it were the middle of the day and she were out shopping for a book, she turned the brass knob and let herself in.

"Hello?" she called, closing the door behind her. When there was no response, she called again, in a more commanding tone this time, "Hello?"

"Be right there," came a distant voice, followed after a time by the leisurely pad of rubber-soled shoes on the back stairs, which was followed, in turn, by John's appearance. At least, it was the appearance of someone she assumed to be John. His face was partially hidden behind the carton he was carrying, a carton that looked to be heavy from the way he carefully lowered it to the ground. When he straightened, he looked her in the eye and said in that slow, quiet way of his, "You're right on time."

For a minute, she didn't speak. The man who had emerged from behind the carton had John's voice and features, but that was the extent of the similarity to the man with whom she served on the Crosslyn Rise consortium. This John's face wasn't pale, but flushed with activity and shadowed with a distinct end-of-the-day beard. This John's face slightly shaggy brown hair was clustered into spikes on his forehead, which glistened with sweat. As she watched, he mopped a trickle of that sweat from his temple, displaying a forearm that was leanly muscular and spattered with hair.

"I aim to please," she said lightly, but she couldn't take her eyes from him.

This time he ran the back of his hand over his upper lip. "I'm short of space up here, so the courier service puts deliveries in the basement. I've been carting books around, trying to get things organized. If I'd realized I was going to build up a sweat, I'd have showered and changed."

"No problem." She was still wearing the red dress she'd had on since dawn. "It's the end of the day. Besides," she added in an attempt to set the tone for their meeting, "we won't be long enough to make it worth the effort. I'm sure we can hash out our differences in no time."

He responded to the suggestion with a nonchalant twitch of his lips. "I don't know about that, but you're welcome to try." Leaning over, he slit the carton open with a single-edged blade, set the blade back on the counter and pulled the flaps up. "Go ahead. I'm listening."

He was wearing the same plaid shirt he'd been wearing that morning, only he'd paired it with jeans. They fit his lean hips so familiarly that his shoulders looked broad. She hadn't expected that. She had thought he'd be spindly under his corduroy blazer. She had also thought he'd be weak, but from the looks of the carton he'd been carrying—and the fact that, though sweaty, he wasn't winded in the least—she'd been wrong. She could see strength in his forearms, in his shoulders, in the denim-sheathed legs that straddled the box as he began to unload it.

Straightening with an armful of books, he looked at her. "I'm listening," he said again, and the mild derision in his eyes wasn't to be mistaken. Only when she saw it, though, did she realize something else.

"You're not wearing your glasses." She'd never seen him without them before, had simply assumed they were a constant.

"They get in the way sometimes."

"Don't you need them to see?"

"When I'm reading. Or driving. Or thinking of doing either." Turning away, he hunkered down by a low riser near the cash register and began to stack the books, turning one right, then one left, alternating until his arms were empty. When he was finished and stood, she realized yet another thing. Though he wasn't tall by the standards of men like Carter Malloy and Gideon Lowe, in relation to her own five foot two, he was long. She guessed him to be just shy of six feet.

"Something wrong?" he asked with maddening calm.

She felt a warm flush creep up from her neck, all the more disconcerting because she wasn't normally one to blush. Rarely did things take her by surprise the way John Sawyer's physical presence had. "No, no. It's just that you look so different. I'm not sure that if I'd walked in here cold, I'd have connected you with the man at the bank."

He considered that for a minute, then shrugged. "Different circumstances. That's all. I'm still the same guy you're gonna have to give a slew of damn good reasons to before I'll agree that those condominiums should be priced out of sight."

His words stiffened her spine, counteracting any softening she'd felt. "Out of sight? A million dollars would be out of sight. Not six hundred thousand."

"You were arguing for six-fifty to seven-fifty."

"The local market supports that."

He held her gaze without a blink. "Are there any other condominiums—not single-family homes, but condominiums—selling in that range around here?"

She didn't have to check her listings. At any given time, she knew the market like the back of her hand. "No, but only because there haven't been any built that would qualify. Crosslyn Rise does. It's spectacular."

He rubbed the bridge of his nose. "Is that reason to price it so high that no one will be able to enjoy it?"

"Plenty of people will be able to enjoy it."

"Not at that price, and if the condos don't sell, you can kiss the shops goodbye. No merchant—least of all me—wants to open up in a ghost town."

"It wouldn't be a ghost town," Nina scoffed, but softly. He'd raised a good point, namely the connection between sales of the condos and success in renting out the shops. Granted, the shops would hardly be relying on the residents alone; none would survive without the patronage of the public, for which purpose public access had been carefully planned. But the public wouldn't be coming to shop if the rest of the place looked deserted.

Returning to his carton, John bent over and filled his arms a second time with books.

Helpless to look away, Nina noticed the way his dark hair fell across his neck, the way the plaid shirt—darkened in random dots of sweat—stretched across his back, the way his fingers closed around book after book. Those fingers were long and blunt tipped. Rather than being delicate, as she'd have assumed a bookworm's to be, they looked as sturdy as the rest of him. She had the sudden impression that his laid-back manner hid a forbidding toughness. If so, she could be in for trouble.

Wanting to avoid that, she gave a little. "Okay. We could set a limit at seven. The smaller units could be in the low sixes, the larger ones closer to six-ninety-five."

John gathered books into his arms until he couldn't hold any more, then moved to the riser and arranged a second pile beside the first.

"John?"

"You're still a hundred grand too high. There's no need to price gouge."

"There's need to make a profit. That's the name of the game."

"Maybe your game," he said complacently, and returned for a third load.

"And not yours? I don't believe that for a minute. You put your own good money into the consortium, and from what I hear, there isn't a whole lot more where that came from."

One book was stacked on another. He neither broke the rhythm nor looked up from his work.

"The only reason," she said slowly, hoping that maybe a man who spoke slowly needed to hear slowly in order to comprehend, "why a man stakes the bulk of his savings on a single project is if he feels he has a solid chance of getting a good return."

John straightened with the last of the books. "Exactly."

She waited for him to go on. When he simply turned and began arranging a third pile by the first two, she moved closer. "The higher we price these units, the greater your return will be. The difference of a hundred-thousand over two dozen condos is two-and-a-half million dollars. That spells a substantial increase in our profit." She frowned. "My Lord, how many of those books do you have?"

"Twenty-five."

"And you really think you'll sell twenty-five at $22.95 a pop? I could believe five, maybe ten or twelve in a community this size. But twenty-five? How can you be so optimistic about books and so pessimistic about condos?"

Taking his time, he finished stacking the books. When he was done, he stood, wiped his palms on his thighs and gave her a patronizing look. "I can be lavish with books because the publishers make it well worth my while. When they're trying to push something, they offer generous deals and incentives. They're pushing this book like there's no tomorrow."

"It stinks."

He shrugged. "Sorry, but that's the way the publishing world works."

"Not the deals. The book. It stinks."

"You've read it?"

For the first time, she had caught him off guard, if the surprised arch of one brow meant something. "Yes, I've read it."

"When? I thought you worked all the time."

"I never said that."

"Sure sounded it from the way you were standing at the bank this morning struggling to squeeze in a single meeting with me."

"This week's worse than most because of the seminar. It's four intensive days—"

"Of what?"

"Classes on commercial real estate transactions. In the past year or two, I've been doing more with stores and office buildings. I've been wanting to take this seminar for six months, but this is the first time it's been offered at a time and place I could handle."

He gave her a long look. "Funny, I assumed you could handle most anything."

"I can," she said without flinching. "But it's a matter of priorities. Let me rephrase what I said. This is the first time the seminar's been offered at a time and place that work into my schedule without totally screwing up everything else."

He gave that brief thought. "So, when do you read?"

"At night. Late."

"When you can't sleep because you've got yourself wound up about everything you should be doing but can't because no one else is awake to do it with you?"

She was about to summarily deny the suggestion when she realized how right he was. Not that she intended to tell him that. "When I can't sleep, it's because I'm not tired."

The look in his eye was doubtful, but he let her claim ride. "And you didn't like this book?"

"I thought it was self-indulgent. Just because an author writes one book that wins the Pulitzer Prize doesn't mean that everything else that author writes is gold, but you'd have thought that from the hype the book was given. So I blame the author for her arrogance and the publisher for his cowardice."

"Cowardice?"

"In not standing up to the author and sending her back to rewrite it. The book *stinks*."

John pondered that. After a minute, he said, "It'll make the bestselling lists."

"Probably."

"And I won't lose a cent."

Given deals and incentives and bestselling status, he was probably right, she mused.

"Out of curiosity, if nothing else," he went on leisurely, "people will buy the book. No one will be broken by $22.95. Readers may be angry, like you are. They may feel gypped. They may even tell their friends not to buy the book, and I may, indeed, have two of these stacks standing here three months from today, just as they are now. But one disappointing book won't hurt my business." His eyes took on a meaningful cast. "At Crosslyn Rise, on the other hand, a thirty-three percent sell rate will hurt and hurt bad."

Nina shook her head. "The analogy's no good. You're comparing apples and oranges—sweet apples and moldy oranges, at that. Crosslyn Rise is quality. This book isn't. No one who buys into the Rise will ever say that it wasn't worth the money. In fact, some of the sales will probably come about by word of mouth, people who buy and are so excited that they spread the excitement."

"People who are stretched tight financially may not be able to feel much excitement."

"People who are stretched tight financially have no business even looking at the Rise, much less buying into it."

John's eyes hardened. "You're tough."

"I'm realistic. The Rise isn't for first-time home owners. It isn't for twenty-five-year-olds who've just gotten married and have twenty thousand to put down on a mortgage that they'll then pay off each month by painstakingly pooling their salaries." She held up a hand, lest he think her a snob. "Listen, I have properties that are less expensive, and I have clients who are looking for that. But those clients aren't looking for Crosslyn Rise, or if they are, they should be awakened to the rude realities of life."

"Which are?"

"Everything costs. *Everything.* If you don't have money in your pocket to pay for what you want or think you need, the cost comes out of your hide and is ten times more painful."

Her words hung in the air. Even more, her tone. It was hard and angry, everything Nina was accused of being from time to time by one detractor or another whose path she crossed. Now she held her breath, waiting for John Sawyer to accuse her of the same.

He didn't say a word. Instead, after studying her for what seemed an infinite stretch, he turned away, bent and swept up the empty carton, and forcibly collapsed it as he walked from the room.

She waited for him to return. Gnawing on her lower lip, she kept her eyes on the door through which he'd gone. His footsteps told her that he'd taken a flight of stairs, leading her to guess he'd returned to the basement, but all was still. She shifted her bag from the left shoulder to the right, shifted her weight from the right foot to the left, finally glanced at her watch. It was after nine-thirty, getting later and later, and they hadn't reached any sort of agreement on Crosslyn Rise.

"John?" she called. When the only thing to greet her was silence, she let out a frustrated sigh. Wasted time drove her nuts, and this meeting spelled wasted time in capital letters. She and John Sawyer had some very basic differences. He was relaxed and easygoing, she was driven. Neither of them was going to change—not that change was called for. All that was called for was some sort of compromise recommendation for the pricing of the units at Crosslyn Rise.

At the sound of a quiet creaking over her head, she looked up. He must have gone upstairs, she realized, probably to check on his son, and she couldn't begrudge him that. It would have been nice if he'd said something, formally excused himself, told her he'd be back shortly, rather than just walking out. She hadn't associated relaxed and easygoing with rude before, nor had she associated rude with John. Slow, mulish, even naive, perhaps. But not rude.

He didn't like her. That explained it, she guessed. The hardness that came to his eyes from time to time when he looked at her spoke clearly of disapproval, which was all the more reason why she should finish her business and leave. She wasn't a glutton for punishment. If he didn't like her, fine. All they needed was to come up with a simple decision, and she'd be gone.

The creaking came again from upstairs, this time more steadily. Soon after, she heard footsteps on the back stairs, but they went on longer than they should have. It didn't take a genius to figure out that he'd gone on down to the basement, and in the wake of that realization, she realized something else. She didn't like John Sawyer any more than he liked her.

Annoyed, she stalked toward the back room, turned a corner until she saw the stairs and called out an impatient, "I haven't got much time, John. Do you think you could come up here and talk this out with me?"

"Be right up," he called nonchalantly. She could well have been the cleaning lady, for all the attention he was giving her.

Spinning on her heel, she returned to the main room of the shop, where, for the first time, she took a good look around. The bookstore took up the entire front portion of the house. Working around tall windows, a fireplace that looked frequently used, a sofa and several large wing chairs, bookshelves meandered through what had once been a living room, parlor and dining room. The overall space wasn't huge, as stores went, but what it lacked in size, it made up for in coziness.

Antsy, Nina began to prowl. Passing a section of reference books, she wandered past one of history books, another of fiction classics, another of humor. As she wandered, her pace slowed. That always happened to her in bookstores and libraries. Whether she intended to or not, she relaxed. Books pacified her. They were nonjudgmental, nondemanding. They could be picked up or put down with no strings attached, and they were always there.

At the shelves holding recent biographies, she stopped, lifted one, read the inside of its jacket. She liked biographies, as was evidenced by the pile of them on her night shelf, waiting to be read. Tempted by this one but knowing that she didn't dare buy another until she'd made some headway with the pile, she replaced the book and moved toward the front of the store. At the cookbooks, she stopped. One, standing face front, caught her eye, a collection of recipes put together by a local women's group. She took it from the shelf and began to thumb through.

"Don't tell me you cook."

Nina's head flew up to find John's expression as wry as his voice, but neither of those things held her attention for long. What struck her most was the surprise she felt—again—at the way he looked. Tall, strong, strangely masculine. She hadn't expected any of those things, much less her awareness of them. The relaxation she'd felt moments before vanished. "Yes, I cook."

He turned to put down another carton where the first had been. Looking back at her, his eyes were shuttered. "You work, you read, you cook. Any other surprises?"

At least they were even, she mused. He surprised her in not being a total wimp, she surprised him in being a businesswoman who cooked. She still didn't understand his dislike for her, but there was no point in pursuing it. Their personal feelings for each other didn't matter. If Crosslyn Rise was the only thing they had in common, so be it.

"It's getting late," she said with studied patience as she watched him bend in half and slash the new carton open. "Do you think you could take a break from that for a few minutes so that we can settle the matter of pricing?"

Straightening slowly, he slipped the blade back onto the counter. In measured cadence, he said, "I've been listening to everything you've said. You're not swaying me."

"Maybe you're not listening with an open mind."

He gave the possibility consideration before claiming, "My mind is always open."

"Okay," she said in an upbeat, "why don't you run *your* arguments by me again?"

He arched a casual brow. "Would it do any good?"

"It might."

After studying her for several long moments, he bent to open the box and began to unload books.

"John," she protested.

"I'm getting my thoughts in order. Give me a minute."

Tempering her impatience, she gave him that. During its course, he carried half a dozen books to one shelf, half a dozen to another. She was beginning to wonder whether he was deliberately dragging out the time, when he came to face her. His skin wore the remnants of a moist sheen, but his eyes were clear.

"I believe," he said slowly and quietly, "that we should keep the pricing down on those units because, one—" he held up a long, straight finger "—we stand a good chance of selling out that way, which in turn will make the shops more appealing both to shopkeepers and to the general public—" he held up a second finger, "two, we'd attract a better balance of buyers, and three, the profit will be more than respectable." He dropped his hand and turned back to the box of books.

"Is that it?"

"That's enough." Hunkering down, he started to fill his arms. "Didn't I win you over?"

"Not quite."

With a sidelong glance, he shot back her own words. "Maybe you're not listening with an open mind."

"I always have an open mind."

"If that were true, you'd have already given in. My arguments make sense."

"Mine are stronger."

"Yours have to do with profit, and profit alone."

She wanted to pull her hair out. "But profit is what this project is *about*!"

"Right, and you could blow it all by getting greedy. The entire project will be jeopardized if we overprice the goods."

"Okay," she said with a sigh, "if the units aren't snapped up in six months or so, we can reduce the price."

He shook his head. "That smacks of defeat, and it'll taint the whole thing. The longer those units sit empty, the worse it'll be." He sighed patiently. "Look, the duck pond will be completed six months before the pine grove, and the meadow six months after that. If we don't sell the duck pond first thing, there's no way the pine grove will sell, and if the pine grove doesn't sell, forget the meadow."

"Okay," Nina said, trying her absolute best to be reasonable, "how about this. How about we price the duck pond in the sixes, then move up into the sevens as we move toward the meadow."

"How about we price the duck pond in the fives, then move up into the sixes as we move toward the meadow." He reached for more books.

Bowing her head, she squeezed her eyes shut and pressed two fingers to her brow. "This isn't going to work."

"It'd work just fine if you'd listen to reason."

Her head came up, eyes open and beseeching. "But I'm the *expert* here. Pricing property is what I do for a living! If I was off the wall, I wouldn't be as successful as I am!"

Arms filled with books, John straightened and gave her a look that was shockingly intense. "You're successful because you push with such force and persistence that you wear people down. But you're barking up the wrong tree when it comes to me. I'm not the type to be worn down."

Nina stared up at him, stunned by the vehemence of his attack and its personal nature. She couldn't believe what she'd heard, couldn't believe the anger that had come from the quiet, contemplative, laid-back bookseller. Swallowing something strangely akin to hurt, she said, "Why do you dislike me? Have I done something to offend you?"

"Your whole *manner* offends me."

"Because I work hard and earn good money? Because I know what I want and fight for it? Or because I'm a woman?" She took a step back. "That's it, isn't it? I'm a strong woman, and you feel threatened."

"I'm not—"

"Don't feel singled out or anything," she said quickly, and held up a hand. "You're not alone. I threaten lots of men. I make them feel like they're not fast enough or smart enough or insightful enough. They want to put me in my place, but they can't."

John's look was disparaging. "I wouldn't presume to know where your place is, and I doubt you do, either. You want to wear the pants in the family, but you're so busy trying to get them to fit that you blow the family part. How old are you?"

"It doesn't matter."

"It does. You should be home having babies."

She stared at him in disbelief, opened her mouth, closed it again. Finally she sputtered out, "Who are you to tell me something like that? You don't know anything about me. You have no idea what makes me tick. And even if you did, these are the 1990s. Women don't stay home and have babies—"

"Some do."

"And some work. It's a personal choice, one for *me* to make."

"Clearly you have."

"Clearly, and if you were any kind of a man, you'd respect that choice." She was suddenly feeling tired. Hitching her bag to the other shoulder, she headed for the door. "I think we've reached a stalemate here. I'll call Carter tomorrow and let him know. There's no way you and I can work together. No way."

"Chicken."

She stopped in her tracks, then turned. "No. I'm being practical. My standing here arguing with you is an exercise in futility. My arguments won't change your mind, any more than yours will change mind. We're deadlocked. So we'll have to do what I wanted to do from the start, let the whole committee hear the arguments and take a vote. And we'll chalk up this time to—to—client development."

"What does that mean?"

"That some day when you're selling this house and you want the bitchiest broker to get the most money for you, you'll give me a call." With that, she tugged open the door and swept out into the night. She was down the wood steps and well along the front walk before she heard her name called.

"Nina?"

"Save it for the bank," she called back without turning, raised a hand in a wave of dismissal and rounded her car.

"Wait, Nina."

She looked up to find John eyeing her over the top of the car.

"Maybe we should try again," he said.

"It'd be a waste of time." Opening the door, she slid behind the wheel.

He leaned down to talk through the open window. "Why don't you give me some time to think."

With one hand on the wheel and one on the ignition, she said, "Buddy, you could think till the cows come home and you wouldn't see things my way."

"Maybe we could meet halfway, you'd come down a little, I'd come up."

That was the only thing that made any sense, she knew, but the idea of meeting John Sawyer again didn't appeal to her in the least. "Why don't you suggest that next Tuesday at the meeting?"

"They're expecting a recommendation from us."

"We can recommend that the consortium take a vote." She started the car.

"Look," he said, raising his voice so that its even timbre carried over the hum of the engine. "It doesn't matter so much to me if they think we couldn't come to some kind of consensus. Hell, I'm just a bookseller who's trying to make a little money by investing in real estate on the side. But you're supposed to be the master of the hard sell. I'd think you'd want to impress those guys at that table in any way you can."

She did. No doubt about it. Staring out the front window into the darkness with both hands on the wheel, she said, "If we can agree right now to go with figures halfway between what you want and what I want, we've got our consensus."

"I think we ought to discuss it."

"That's the only solution."

"I still think we ought to discuss it."

Earlier, she had thought him mulish. She thought it again now. John had to be one of the most stubborn men she had met in years. Turning her head only enough to meet his gaze, she said, "That sounds just fine, only there's one small problem. We went through the whole week this morning, and the only time we both had free was tonight. Now tonight's gone. So what do you suggest?"

"We find another time."

She shook her head. "Bad week."

"Then the weekend."

"I told you. I have a seminar. It runs from nine to five every day, and I'll have to allow an hour before and after for travel."

"So you'll be home by six. We can meet then."

Again she shook her head. "I'm moving a week from Monday. Every night after the seminar is reserved for packing. I have to get it done."

"I'll help you pack."

Like hell he would. Eyes forward, she set her chin. "No."

"Why not?"

"Because I can do it myself."

"Of course you can," he said indulgently. "But I can help. I'm not the scrawny weakling you imagined I'd be."

Her eyes shot to his. "I never said—"

"But you thought. So you were wrong. And I can help you pack."

"You can *not*. I don't want your help. I don't *need* your help."

He was silent then, his expression a mystery in the dark. Finally, sounding even-tempered and calm, the John she'd known from the bank, he said, "Tuesday morning before the meeting. I'll meet you at Easy Over at seven-thirty. We'll talk over breakfast." Before she could say a word, he gave the side of the car a tap and was off.

"John!" she called after him, but she might just as well have saved her breath. He didn't move quickly, but he moved smoothly, covering the distance to the house and disappearing inside without a glance behind.

3

NINA PREPARED CAREFULLY for breakfast Tuesday morning. After wading through her wardrobe and discarding anything red, purple or lime green, she chose a beige suit that was as reserved as anything she owned. That wasn't to call it conservative. The blazer was nipped in at the waist over a skirt that was short and scalloped, exposing a whisper of thigh with every move. In an attempt to tone that down, she left the matching, low-cut gauzy blouse in her closet in favor of a higher necked silk. With a single strand of pearls around her neck and pearl studs at her ears, she felt she looked as traditional as it was possible for Nina Stone to look.

Her goal was to impress John Sawyer—not in any sort of romantic way, because she *certainly* didn't think of John that way, but in a business way. Normally she dressed in the bright, chic, slightly funky style that had become her trademark; clients came to her because they saw someone who was one step ahead of the eight ball. Somehow she didn't think that was where John Sawyer wanted to be, but she wanted him to be on her side when it came to marketing Crosslyn Rise, so it behooved her to impress him.

She arrived at Easy Over, a light-breakfast and lunch place not far from the bank, at seven-thirty on the dot. When she saw no sign of John, she took a table, ordered a pot of coffee and waited. He arrived five minutes later, wearing loose khaki pants, another plaid shirt, a slouchy brown blazer and glasses. Looking slightly sleepy, he slid into a chair.

"Sorry," he murmured. "Had a little trouble getting out." His eyes fastened on the coffeepot. "Is that fresh?"

She nodded, lifted the pot and filled the cup waiting by his place. "Anything serious?"

"Nah." He took a sip of coffee, then a second before setting down the cup, sitting back in his chair and catching her eye. "That's better. I didn't have time for any at home."

"What happened?"

He took another drink, a more leisurely one this time as though he were just then settling in to being his normal slow self. "My son isn't wild about the sitter. He didn't want me to leave."

"I thought kids nowadays were used to sitters. Don't you have one every day?"

"He likes the afternoon ones. They're high school girls with lots of energy and enthusiasm. For morning meetings at the bank, I have to use someone else. She's kind enough, and responsible, but she doesn't relate so well with him."

"He must be very attached to you."

"I'm all he has."

Nina thought about the boy's mother, wondered how she had died and whether the child remembered her. She wasn't about to ask John any of those things, though. They weren't her business.

"What'll it be, folks?" the waitress asked, flipping the paper on her pad and readying a pen.

Nina didn't have to look at the menu. She'd been at Easy Over enough to know what was good. "I'll have Ronnie's Special. Make the eggs soft-boiled, the bacon crisp and the wheat toast dry. And I'll have a large TJ with that." She watched the waitress note everything, then turned expectant eyes toward John.

He hadn't opened the menu either, but he seemed thoughtful for a minute. "Make that two," he paused, "only I want my eggs scrambled, my sausages moist and my rye toast with butter."

"Juice?" the waitress prompted.

"OJ. Large." Still writing, the waitress ambled off. John turned placid eyes on Nina. "For a little girl, you eat a whole lotta food."

"I have to. I rarely make it to lunch, and dinner won't be until eight or nine tonight."

"That's not healthy."

She shrugged. "Can't be helped. I'm into my busiest season. If I don't make the most of it, it'll be gone, and then where will I be?" With the reminder, she pulled up the folder that had been waiting against the leg of her chair, set it down in front of her and opened it up. "I spent awhile yesterday working with figures." She lifted the first sheet from the folder, but before she could pass it to him, he held up a hand.

"Not yet."

"Not yet?"

"Not before breakfast." He settled more comfortably in his seat. "I can't deal with business before breakfast."

"But this is a *business* breakfast. That means we eat while we talk."

His gaze touched the clean white Formica surface before him. "We haven't got any food yet. Let's wait on business."

Nina wanted to say that if they did that, they would not only be wasting good time, but if she had to go past

Plan A to Plan B or C, they might well run *out* of time before they reached an agreement. She wanted to say that first thing in the morning was the *best* time to discuss business, while they were the freshest. She wanted to say that they were due at the bank at eight-thirty, which, given John's tardiness and the time they'd already spent in chitchat and ordering, left them not much more than forty-five minutes.

She didn't say any of those things, because John's eye stopped her. She saw something in them, something strong enough to penetrate his glasses, something with a quiet but forceful command. She also saw that his eyes were amber, then looked more carefully and didn't see it at all. She remembered it. It must have registered on her subconscious the last time she'd seen him.

Carefully, with her heart beating a hair faster than it had been moments before, she set down the paper, sat back in her chair, crossed her hands in her lap and wondered what they would talk about in the time before their food arrived. There were a million things she could ask him, things she was curious about, like his wife and his son and his interest in books. Only none of that was her business.

She was used to talking. She *always* talked. Her role in life was to keep things moving, to win people over, to make sales. But she didn't know what to say to John.

She was beginning to feel awkward—and annoyed at that—when he asked, "Did you get your packing done?"

Relieved, she nodded. "Most of it."

"I trust you had other people to help you."

"No."

He arched a questioning brow and shook his head. She shook her head right back.

"No stream of admirers dying to show off their muscles?"

His tone was deferential, his expression benign. Still she had the feeling that somewhere inside he harbored a grudge. "No stream of admirers. No men at all. Why would you think that there were?"

"You're an attractive woman. You must have men all over you."

"I'm an *independent* woman. I couldn't bear to have men all over me. I told you I didn't need anyone's help."

"You told me you didn't need *my* help."

"Then you took it too personally. I didn't—don't— need anyone's help. When I do, I hire it and pay for it. By check," she tacked on, just so he didn't think she was trading her body for something. Men tended to think that way, and she hated it. The few men—precious few men—she'd been with in her thirty-one years had known that she gave because she felt affection and attraction, and because she knew they wouldn't demand anything more. They never did. She was as free as a bird, and glad of it.

"Where are you moving to?"

"Sycamore Street."

His brow flickered into a frown. "I go down Sycamore all the time. I don't remember seeing any For Sale signs—or were you able to get an inside scoop and snatch something up before it hit the open market?"

There it was again, the deferential tone, the benign look, the little dig underneath. Looking him straight in those amber eyes of his, she said, "I'm not buying. I'm renting the second floor of a duplex, and, yes, I snatched it up before it hit the market. That's one of the perks of being a broker, and it's perfectly legal."

She had been direct enough to issue a challenge and expected him to meet it. Instead, he simply looked surprised. "You're renting? I'd have thought a successful woman like you would be living in a spectacular house on a spectacular piece of land with a spectacular view of the ocean."

"I'm not that successful. Not yet." But she intended to be. One day, she'd have enough money to buy anything her heart desired. "Where I live right now isn't as important as saving as much money as I can."

"You put a whole lot into Crosslyn Rise."

"No more than you." They'd each seen the figures.

"That's a whole lot."

She thought about the sum. "Uh-huh."

"And you want to open your own business."

Her brow went up. "Who told you that?"

"Carter," he answered factually. "When the consortium was forming. Just like he told you about me. So when do you think you'll do it?"

"I don't know. It depends on how much money we make on Crosslyn Rise and how soon." Her hand went to the first paper on her pile, but before she could address herself to its contents, the waitress placed a large glass of tomato juice in front of her. She smiled her thanks and opened her mouth to speak to John when he stopped her with a hand.

"Not yet. I need food first."

"There's food," she said, pointing to his orange juice. "Drink up, then I'll talk."

Rather than taking a drink of the orange juice, though, he drained the last of his coffee and refilled the cup. "Aren't you happy at Crown?"

After a moment's consideration, she gave a one-shouldered shrug. "As happy as I'd be working for someone else, but I've always wanted to be on my own."

"Independent."

"That's right."

"So you can rake in the most bucks?"

She raised her chin. "It's not as much the money as the freedom. I don't like having to answer to someone else."

"Marty Crown's a nice guy."

"A very nice guy. I could have done a lot worse picking a boss." Not that she'd left that to chance. Before moving up from New York she had researched each and every real estate agency in the North Shore area. She'd picked Crown for its reputation, its connections and Martin.

"Does he know your plans?"

"No, and I'd rather he not," she advised, sending John a look that said she was trusting him to keep her secret. "I've done well for Martin in the six years I've been here. He's made good money from my sales, and I don't begrudge that. It's the way things work. He gets his share in exchange for giving me a forum to work and to learn. I'm a much better broker now than I was when I came. Whether I have Martin to thank for that, or myself, isn't important. What's important is that if I can take out of Crosslyn Rise double what I put in, I'll be in great shape to make my move." Feeling that to be as smooth a segue as any, she once again fingered the top sheet in her file.

Once again John stalled her. "That's a lot of money," he said with thought-filled preponderance. "I'd have thought you could pretty much set up a real estate brokerage wherever you wanted with little more than a telephone."

"Not the kind of brokerage I want," she said, and let her dreams momentarily surface. "I want something classy. I want to either buy a house and do it over, or rent the best commercial space available. Then I want to decorate with the best furnishings, the best window treatments, the best artwork. I want a secretary, a sophisticated telephone system to make certain parts of my work easier, a computer setup to handle the latest programs and handle them well. I want to design a distinctive logo and stationery, and I want to advertise." She took a breath. "All of that costs money."

"I'll say," John said, and sat quietly back, studying her as though she were something foreign that he couldn't quite understand. "Couldn't you start small? Do you need everything all at once?"

"Yes. That's the whole point. Real estate agencies are a dime a dozen around here. Granted, some are better than others, and those stand out. But for a new one to spring up and attract enough of a clientele to be successful, drastic measures are called for. From the very first, my agency has to be different. It has to attract attention. I think I can do it if, A, my offices are elegant, B, my staff is courteous, hardworking and smart, and, C, I advertise like hell."

"Your staff?"

She sent him a dry look. "I'm not doing all the work on my own. That would be suicide. The whole point is to have people who are answerable to me, to teach them and train them, let them do their work; then take *my* cut in the profits. Isn't that the way successful entrepreneurs do it?"

John didn't answer. He took a slow drink of his juice, set it down, then pushed his utensils out of the way when the waitress delivered plates filled with eggs, meat and toast.

Mindful that once they had food in their stomachs, John would be willing to talk business, Nina began to eat. She cracked her eggs, scooped them from the shell onto the wheat toast, gave them a light sprinkling of salt.

John's fork seemed stuck in the first of his scrambled eggs. "I'm surprised," he said unhurriedly, "that you want to set up business around here. If the goal is to make money and buy your freedom—"

"Not buy. Ensure."

"Ensure. If that's what you want, wouldn't you be better in a large place where, by virtue of sheer numbers of people, the market would be more active?"

"I've been there. I didn't like it."

"Why not?"

"Too impersonal. I may be hard, driven, aggressive, ambitious, even ruthless—people have called me all those things—but I like being able to greet the local grocer by name and have him greet me the same way. Besides," she added with a glance out the window, "I do love the ocean."

John followed her gaze briefly before returning to her. "When do you have time to see it?"

"I see it. Here and there. Coming and going." She nudged her chin toward his plate. "Eat up. Time's passing."

"Ever spend a day at the beach?"

"A day? No. An hour or two, maybe. Any more and I get itchy."

"You never wanted just to lie out on the sand for hours listening to the sound of people and the surf?"

"No. There's too much to do."

He took a bite of his eggs, then swallowed. "That's sad."

"Maybe for you. Not for me. I'd much rather get brief glimpses of the ocean lots of different times in the course of a day, know that it's there, even listen to it at night at the same time that I'm getting something else useful done, than sit doing nothing on the sand."

He looked baffled. "But don't you ever just want to go out and enjoy it for itself, rather than as an accompaniment to something else?"

"Why should I? It's the best accompaniment in the world. It makes anything else I'm doing that much nicer."

"That's sad," he said again, and Nina found herself getting irked.

"I don't see *you* with a tan."

"I haven't had time yet this spring. But I will. You can count on it. As soon as lessons let up a little for my son, we'll be hitting the beach."

Nina was about to ask what lessons he meant, when she caught herself. The child had a handicap. She didn't want to put John on the spot. Besides, his personal life wasn't her affair.

With a tolerant shrug, she said, "Different strokes for different folks. What works for you doesn't necessarily work for me, and vice versa. It's no big thing, John. Really." He didn't believe her, but that wasn't her worry. Crosslyn Rise was. "Listen, I'd really like to get to those papers." She glanced at her watch. "We have to be at the bank in less than half an hour."

"How was your seminar?"

"My seminar was fine." She put her hand on the top paper. "What I have here is my personal recommendation. I've broken the project down by size and expected date of completion—"

"Did you learn a lot? At the seminar."

She paused, stared, nodded. Then she patted the paper. "The more I thought about it over the weekend, the more I realized that we hit on something good last time we talked. The idea of—"

"Was it worth the four days?"

She took a breath for patience. "I'd say so."

"You're a better broker for it?"

"I'm more knowledgeable." She took another breath. "The idea of pricing the units progressively—"

"Don't you ever get tired?"

She pressed her lips together. "Of work? I told you. I love my work."

"But don't you ever get *tired*?"

"You mean physically fatigued?"

"Mentally fatigued. Don't you ever want to stop, even for a little while?"

"If I do that, it'll take me longer to reach my goal."

"What about burnout?"

"What about it?"

"Doesn't it scare you?"

"Not particularly. If I get where I'm going, I'll have plenty of time to take it easy, without the risks."

"What are the risks?"

"Of taking it easy now?" She didn't have to take time to think. She lived with certain fears day in, day out. "Loss of sales. Loss of reputation. Loss of status in the agency. There are other brokers out there just dying for my listings. If I'm not around, if I'm not working, if I'm not on top of things, if I'm not getting results, I lose."

In a rare instance of expressiveness, his mouth twisted in disgust. "I get tired just listening to you."

"Then don't," she snapped. "Don't ask me questions, and you won't have to listen to my answers. All I want—" she slapped the paper beside her plate "—is to come to some sort of decision here!"

John stared at her. She glared back. Gradually his stare softened into study, and before she knew it, she felt the same kind of quiet force emanating from him that she'd felt before. As had happened then, her heartbeat picked up, all the more so when his amber eyes began a slow, almost tactile meandering over her face. She felt their touch on her cheeks, her nose, her chin, then her mouth, where they lingered for a while to trace the bow curve of her lips.

The indignation she felt moments earlier was forgotten, pushed from mind by a strange, all-over tingle. "John?" Her voice wobbled. She cleared her throat. "I, uh, really think we should talk."

He wasn't done, though. His gaze dropped to her throat, touching the smooth skin there before slipping down over silk to the gentle swell of her breasts.

Even sitting, she felt weak in the knees, which made so little sense at all that a flare of pique shot through her. "John."

His eyes rose. "Hmm?"

"I *need* to show you my *papers*."

"What papers?"

She rapped the folder. "*These*."

He looked at the folder, then looked back at her. Along the way, his mouth hardened. "You won't let it go, will you?"

"Let it go? But this is why we met!"

He said nothing, just stared at her. Not even his glasses diffused the strength of that stare.

She felt penetrated. "Wasn't it?"

Slowly he shook his head.

"Then why?"

"To have breakfast."

"You insisted on this meeting just for *breakfast*?"

Slowly he nodded.

"But *why*? You could have had breakfast for less money and with less hassle if you'd stayed home with your son. Why on *earth* did you drag me out here if you didn't have any intention of discussing Crosslyn Rise?"

"We'll discuss Crosslyn Rise. When we're done eating."

"So what do I do until then?" she asked in exasperation.

"You slow down. You take a deep breath. You look out that window and watch the sea gulls. You have a second cup of coffee and take the time to smell the brew." His voice lowered, growing sharper and more direct. "You're rushing your way through life, Nina. If you're not careful, the whole thing will be over and you won't know what in the hell you've missed."

Incredulity holding her mute, Nina stared. She had to take a deep, deep breath and give a solid swallow before she was able to say, "Last time I looked, this was my life. Seems to me I should be able to do what I want, and if that means rushing, I'll rush."

His voice came out gentler than before, but no less direct. "Not with me, you won't."

She sat back in her chair. "Fine." Two could play the game. She hadn't wanted this breakfast, anyway. All along, she had wanted the committee to take its vote. "Fortunately, I won't *be* with you beyond this meeting." She smiled. "Take your time. Eat. I'll just sit here and enjoy the scenery."

SHE WORKED HARD at doing that. After an eternity, with barely ten minutes until they were due at the bank, John invited her to show him the papers she'd brought. Staying calm, patient and professional, she went through them. With surprising ease, they came to an agreement on the third of her plans. Together they walked to the bank.

Sixty minutes later, when Nina returned to her office, she was like a steam kettle ready to blow. Slapping the folder sharply on her desk, she squeezed her eyes shut, put her head back and let out an eloquent growl. Its sound brought Lee in from next door.

"How'd it go?"

"Don't ask."

"Which plan did he go for?"

"C, damn it."

"And the consortium agreed?"

Nina nodded. Seconds later, she threw a hand in the air. "Don't ask me why I didn't argue more. I should have."

"Plan C is just fine."

"It's not aggressive enough."

"So why *didn't* you argue more?"

"Because—because—" she struggle for the words, finally blurting out, "because John Sawyer wore me down, that's why."

"I thought he was *blah*."

"He is."

"But he wore you down." Lee grinned in a curious kind of way. "That's a change. Usually it's the other way around. You must be losing your touch." When Nina gave her a dirty look, she said in an attempt to appease, "Sometimes the most blah people can be forceful, just because they take you by surprise."

But it wasn't that, Nina knew. It was John's persistence, his molasses-slow approach and a doggedness that was built of reason. His will was stronger than she'd expected, and, as fate would have it, his will coincided with that of the majority of the consortium.

Not for the first time, Nina vowed that she would never again involve herself in a project where decisions were made by committee. Unfortunately, she was stuck with this one to the end. "Crosslyn Rise may be the death of me yet." Snatching up the pink slips that were waiting, she flipped sightlessly through, then flattened them back on the desk. "The *worst* of it is that they want me to keep working with him. Can you believe that? They see him as kind of a lay advisor. So even though consortium meetings won't be held more than once a month through the summer, they're expecting John and I to meet once a week."

"That shouldn't be too hard."

"It's a royal waste of time, a total frustration." She sent a beseeching look skyward. "Someone up there better help me out, or I'll be a raving lunatic by the time summer's done." Eyes dropping back to the desk, she sighed. "At least I can give the printer the go-ahead to print those brochures." Moving the folder aside, she drew up a pad of paper. At the top, she wrote Call Printer. "I want to have an introductory Open House over the Fourth of July weekend, something with lots of hoopla to launch the selling campaign." To the list, she added, Call Christine, then Call Newspaper. Her pen went back to the Christine part. "*If* the model apartment is ready. Chris was aiming for the first of the month. It'll be impressive." Looking at Lee, she asked, "Have you been up there lately?"

Lee shook her head. "I'm waiting for you. Maybe today, after lunch?"

Something about the way Lee mentioned lunch gave Nina pause. She dropped her eyes to her desk calendar. Catching in a breath, she said, "Lunch! That's right!" She had forgotten all about it. With a grin, she looked up. "Happy birthday, Lee."

Lee blushed. "Thanks."

"I'm sorry. Wow, I should have been thinking about that when you first walked in here, but I've been so annoyed all morning. Hey, how does it feel to be twenty-nine?"

"You've been there. How did it feel to you?"

"I don't know. It came and went so fast, I think I missed it." For a split second, she remembered what John Sawyer had said, then pushed her mind on to more meaningful things. "So, we'll go out for lunch to celebrate. Any other plans?"

"I'm meeting my parents in town for dinner."

"Nice," Nina said with enthusiasm, though she couldn't help but wonder about Tom Brody. If there was something real going on between Tom and Lee, he should have been the one to take her to dinner on her birthday.

As though reading her mind, Lee said, "Tom and I celebrated last night." She touched her earlobe. "See?"

Nina was a stickler for her own appearance, dressing for the part she wanted to play. She carefully shopped for clothes and accessories, and wore them unselfconsciously once they were hers. There, though, her interest in fashion ended. She was far more apt to notice the overall effect of a person's clothing than the details of it. That was why she hadn't noticed Lee's earrings before.

Looking back, she didn't know how she'd missed them. They lit up Lee's ears in a way that neither gold, silver nor neon enamel could. "Wow," she breathed, coming out of her chair for a closer look. "Those are *gorgeous*."

"They're three-quarters of a karat each. Tom said to make sure I insured them."

Nina wanted to say that if Tom Brody had style, he'd have given her a year's worth of insurance along with the gift. But Tom had flash, not style. There was a difference.

"Definitely insure them," Nina said. She didn't add that that way Lee would be sure to have something of value when Tom left her behind. Nina wasn't a spoiler. But she felt awful. "It's too bad he can't join you tonight. Has he ever met your parents?"

"No. He has to be in Buffalo. It's just as well," Lee reasoned indulgently. "My parents would be looking Tom over as husband material, and that kind of pressure is the last thing Tom needs. He has enough pressure with work."

Nina felt momentarily chilled. Making excuses for a man was a sure sign that a woman was giving more than she was getting. But before she could say that, Lee made for the door.

"Martin is having a root canal. I told him I'd cover for him. He has some people coming in from the Berkshires. Their daughter is starting at Salem State in the fall and they want to buy a condo for the four years she's here."

Nina was hearing that same story more and more often. She supposed that if she had kids she'd want to do the same thing, since, given rents versus tax benefits and property appreciation, it made sense. Of course, she didn't have kids, so it was a moot point.

"How about I make reservations for twelve-thirty?" she asked.

"Sounds great," Lee said. "I'll be back here by twelve. See you then."

Nina waved a goodbye, then looked again at her desk calendar. The fact that she'd forgotten about lunch was nothing new. At the end of a given day, when she looked over her program for the next one, business appointments were the things she saw. Fortunately, she didn't have anything that would conflict with Lee's birthday celebration. She liked Lee a lot. She felt good about taking her out.

She was also grateful for the opportunity to eat, since she hadn't had much of the breakfast she had so glibly ordered at Easy Over. John had distracted her. Even when he'd been leisurely eating his own food, she hadn't eaten much. He made her stomach jump.

Annoyance, she told herself. Annoyance and irritation. John was the kind who, in his innocent way, gave people ulcers.

Actually, it was a wonder he was so calm, given the problem he had with his son. It couldn't be easy for him raising a child alone. She wondered about the extent of the boy's problems, wondered what kind of schooling those problems entailed. She wondered whether John ever got frantic, threw his hands into the air and gave up. Some parents did that when confronted with a frightening situation. Her mother had, more than once.

Something nagged in the back of her mind. Lifting the collection of pink slips that she'd barely seen earlier, she set one after another aside until she came to the one that had caused the nagging. It was a message from Anthony Kimball, the medical director of the Omaha nursing home where her mother lived. The call had come in promptly at nine that morning. The message requested a callback.

Lifting the phone, Nina punched out the number that she knew by heart. "Dr. Kimball, please," she asked. She gave her name, then waited while the call was transferred.

"Nina?"

"Yes, Dr. Kimball. I got your message. Is something wrong?" It wasn't often that Anthony Kimball called her, and when he did, there was usually a problem.

"I'm not quite sure. Your mother had some sort of seizure during the night. Her blood pressure fell dangerously low. We have her stabilized now, and there doesn't seem to be any other side effect from whatever the seizure was, but I thought you ought to know. This may be the start of the weakening that we've been expecting."

Nina swiveled her chair away from the door and bowed her head. "Is she comfortable?" she asked quietly.

"As far as we can tell."

"Is she aware of anything?"

There was a pause, then a quiet, "I don't believe so."

Nina sighed. "I guess we should be grateful for that." She pressed a hand to her eyes. "This weakening. Once it begins, does it go fast?"

"I can't tell you that. Every case varies. It could take one month or ten, but you may want to come out here to see her within the next few weeks."

Nina didn't have to look at her calendar to know that the next few weeks were fully booked. This was her busy season. A trip to Omaha would take precious time, not to mention a toll on her emotions. Seeing her mother was always painful. "Why don't I talk with you next week and see how she is then," she suggested. "If she stays stabilized, I'd rather wait a bit before coming out."

The doctor agreed to that, as Nina knew he would. Though the home was the finest Nina had been able to find, it wasn't unlike others in its overriding concern with money. Nina paid well for the service of having her mother cared for. As long as the checks kept coming, Anthony Kimball and his staff were content.

Hanging up the phone, Nina felt the same hollow ache she felt whenever she thought of her mother. Such potential gone to waste. A beautiful woman now a vegetable. She wished she could credit the damage to a disease like Alzheimer's, but her mother's mind hadn't fallen victim to anything as noble as that. She'd taken drugs. Bad drugs. Too many drugs. Rather than dying of an overdose, she had lived on, simply to languish in whatever position her attendants arranged her.

Nina was the one who felt the pain of it all. She was the one who felt the remorse. She couldn't say that she felt a loss, because her mother had never been hers to enjoy, but there were times, once in a very great while, when she thought of what might have been if things had been different way back at the start.

But they wouldn't be—couldn't be—and thinking about it only caused pain. One of Nina's earliest lessons in life had been that the only sure antidote to pain was activity. It was a lesson she still lived by.

4

Sunday was moving day. Nina completed all her weekend showings on Saturday and was up with the sun the next morning to pack the last of her things. Rather than pay a formal moving service, when she had so little of intrinsic value to move, she had hired two young men to help. Between their muscles, the small pickup truck one of them owned and the promise of a generous check for the job, they had successfully transferred her meager furnishings and not so meager personal belongings from the old apartment to the new one by noon.

Shortly after, Nina went to work, first pushing the furniture over or back until the positioning was perfect, then opening carton after carton in an attempt to see what was where. She was standing in the midst of chaos, feeling vaguely bewildered, when she heard a call from downstairs.

"Hello?"

She tried to place it, but she wasn't expecting any guests. "Yes?" she called back without moving.

"It's John Sawyer, Nina. Can I come up?"

"Uh—" she looked around, bewildered, "—sure." John Sawyer? Downstairs? She hadn't seen hide nor hair of him since the Tuesday before, and though she told herself to be grateful, more than once she had wondered where he was. The consortium wanted them to work together, but since she wasn't thrilled with the idea, she'd decided to leave the initiative up to him. She hadn't expected that he'd seek her out in person, much less at her home, much *less* at the home whose exact address he couldn't possibly have known.

Yet John Sawyer it was emerging from the stairwell wearing a T-shirt, jeans and sneakers. His hair was mussed, his nose and cheeks unexpectedly ruddy. He looked fresh and carefree, neither of which she was feeling at that moment, and as if that weren't bad enough, the first thing he did after he came to a halt was to give her an ear-to-ear grin.

John had never grinned at her before. She'd caught a twist of the corner of the mouth once or twice, but never a full-fledged grin. The surprise of it had her insides doing little flip-flops, to which she responded by frowning.

"How did you find me?"

"Your car. You said you were moving to Sycamore Street. There aren't many houses here with bright red BMWs in the driveway."

For reasons unknown to Nina just then, she felt suddenly defensive about the car. "It's not new. I bought it used and had it painted. Some people think it's pretentious to have a car like that when I live pretty modestly, but the fact is that it impresses clients. They like riding around in it."

John studied her, his grin softening into something curious. "Don't you?"

"Don't I what?"

"Like riding around in it."

"I suppose." She frowned again. "What are you doing here?"

"Helping." He stuck his hands into the back pockets of his jeans, a gesture that should have been totally innocent. Given the way his T-shirt tightened over his chest, though, it wasn't. Nina felt a corresponding tightening in the pit of her stomach.

"I told you I didn't need help," she snapped, scowling now.

"Everyone needs help." His eyes skimmed the sea of cartons on the floor. "This place will be a mess until everything's unpacked. Why be burdened doing it after work every day this week, when between the two of us, we can get it all done now?"

He had a point, though she wouldn't concede it. "I'm sure you have better things to do with your time."

"Actually, I don't. J.J. and I were at the beach this morning, but he's gone off for the afternoon with friends, and the store is closed, so I really do have time to waste. I'm in the mood for unpacking." Shifting his hands from his pockets to his hips, he looked around at the cartons. "Where should I begin?"

"Uh—" Nina tried to concentrate, but all she could think about was that she hadn't showered, that she hadn't put makeup on and that between her ultrashort hair and the loose shirt and jeans she wore, she looked more like a boy than a girl. She felt embarrassed. "Uh, really, John, there's no need—"

"Where?" he repeated. Stepping over one carton, he peered down to look at the writing on the side of another. The words *living room* had been crossed out and replaced by *dining room*, but that, too, had been crossed out. *Bedroom* was the word that seemed left, though even from where she was, Nina saw through the open flaps of the box that it contained pots and pans.

"I've used these cartons lots of different times," she explained, wringing one hand in the other. "I kind of gave up on marking things this time, which is why everything's mixed up out here."

"No sweat," John said, lifting the carton. "This looks like it goes in the kitchen." He hitched his chin toward the back of the house. "That way?"

"Uh-huh."

Carrying the carton, he passed her, went through the dining room and into the kitchen. Within minutes, she heard the clattering of pots and pans being stacked. Wondering where he was putting them, she followed the noise to find him on his haunches before one of the kitchen cabinets. "I don't know if this is right, but at least they'll be out of the way. If you find in a week or a month that you want them elsewhere, it'll be easy enough to move them."

"That's fine."

"Why don't you go back into the other room and sort through the rest of the cartons. If I carry stuff into the bedroom, you can organize things there, while I finish up here."

She tried again. "John, this really isn't necessary."

"Of course, it's not. But it helps, doesn't it?"

Given the direct question, she couldn't lie. "Yes, but—"

"Unless there's stuff here you don't want me to see."

"There isn't, but—"

"Or you're expecting someone else and my being here will embarrass you—"

"I'm not and it won't, but—"

"Then there's no problem."

"There *is* a problem," she cried, driven by exasperation to a semblance of her usual force. "I told you this last week. If I wanted help, I'd hire it."

He looked up at her. "And pay for it. With a check. Yes, I did hear that."

"Well, I meant it."

His eyes held hers for a time before he returned them to the task at hand. He had barely set another pot into the nest of them in the cabinet when he looked up again. "This is free, Nina. I'm not asking for payment of any kind, and if you offered, I'd give it back. I'm doing this as a friend. You won't owe me anything."

She felt color warm her cheeks. "I know that."

"I'm not sure you do," he said with a frown. "You've made it clear that you prefer to hire and pay people when you need things done. But when you get someone who's willing to help for free, the only reason I can think of why you'd turn him down is that either you can't stand his company or you're afraid there's a price." His words came slowly but steadily, one sentence flowing gently into the next. "Now, I know we haven't necessarily hit it off on a personal basis, so it may well be that you can't stand my company, and if that's the case, just tell me, and I'll leave. On the other hand, if you're afraid there's a price, I'm telling you there isn't. I'm offering my services free and clear of return obligations." He paused. "Do you believe me?"

After a minute, she said a quiet, "Yes."

"Then why don't you let me help." It was more statement than question. "Come on, Nina. Go with the flow. I'm here and I'm willing. Use me."

Use me. It was usually the other way around, where relationships between men and women were concerned. But he'd said the words himself. He'd offered them. Freely. Just as he was offering his help. "Are you sure you don't have anything else to do?"

"I'm sure."

As he sat there on his haunches looking up at her, it struck Nina that he wasn't bad looking. Not bad looking at all. Actually, rather good-looking, even with those glasses perched on his nose. With his longish hair, his light tan, and his T-shirt and jeans, the glasses made him look oddly in vogue.

Which was a surprising thought, indeed.

"Fine," she said, and headed for the front room before she had a chance to regret the decision. "I'll sort through the cartons. Come back in when you need another one."

With a certain amount of kicking and shoving, she had cartons separated into groups by the time John returned. As promised, he carried everything for the bedroom into the bedroom before continuing with the kitchen.

For one hour, then a second, they worked straight. Nina was back to being her usual efficient self, in part to keep her mind occupied and away from the fact of John's presence in the other room. Come the time when they were both unpacking cartons in the living room, that became more difficult. He was never out of sight. She was highly aware of him. Adding to the problem, most of the cartons contained books, so John's progress slowed. For every four that he placed on the shelf, there was one that he wanted to discuss.

She tried to keep moving. She tried, even when she was giving her opinion of one book or another, to keep unloading others and lining them up on the shelves. But the questions he asked were good ones, often ones that required thought, and she found her own progress slowing down right along with his. She found herself curious to know *his* opinions.

Nina had never thought of herself as an intellectual. She had a college degree more out of practical necessity than love of learning. John, on the other hand, was an intellectual. It was clear in the way he looked and acted, not to mention his occupation, and to some extent, she had assumed that given this difference between them, they would have trouble communicating. To her surprise, they didn't. He didn't make obscure references to classical writers or philosophers. He didn't pick apart books along the lines of arcane theories. He offered honest, straightforward thoughts in honest, straightforward English. Pleasantly surprised, she indulged herself the discussion, letting her defenses down, enjoying the talk for talk's sake.

Engrossed as she was in it, she was taken off guard when, in the midst of a discussion of James Joyce and his wife, Nora, John said, "Have you had lunch?"

Sitting cross-legged on the floor, she straightened, looked at him, swallowed. Dragging herself back from a pleasant interlude to the present, she glanced at her watch. "It's after three."

"I know. I'm starved. Did you have anything?"

Silently she shook her head.

"I'll go get something." Coming to his knees, he fished his keys from his pocket. With another smooth motion, he was on his feet. "You'll eat, won't you?"

"I don't need—"

"Are you hungry?"

"I wasn't planning to—"

"Lobster rolls?"

Her mouth watered. "Only if I pay."

He thought about that for a minute. She was prepared to dig in her heels and insist that that was the only way she'd eat anything he brought, when his mouth quirked. "Okay."

He was *quite* good-looking, she realized with a start. Dragging her eyes from his, she looked around for her purse. Unfortunately, it was directly behind him. The only footpath through the cartons took her by him with mere inches to spare. His flesh was warm from work. She felt that warmth, smelled its scent, and where she should have been repelled, she wasn't. John Sawyer smelled healthily male. Attractively male.

Convinced that the tension of the move was jumbling her mind, she quickly found her purse and fumbled inside her enough money to cover sandwiches and drinks. John took the money.

"You do know," he said, and eyed her straight on, "that I'd never allow this if it weren't for the big deal you made about not wanting my help to unpack. The way I see it, your treating me now is payment for my work, so we're even. Got that?"

His gaze was so strong and his voice so firm that all she could do was manage a quiet, "Uh-huh." If he had asked her to say anything else, she'd have been at a loss. Fortunately, he didn't. Tucking the money into his pocket, he went off down the stairs.

During the time he was gone, Nina was a whirling dervish of activity. Bending over and around repeatedly, she emptied two full cartons of books, then moved on to her stereo equipment. She tried not to think about anything but the work she was doing, and to some extent she succeeded. Only intermittently did images flash through her mind—John's long arms flexing under the weight of cartons, John's shaggy hair spiking along his neck, John's very male, very alluring scent—but she pushed them away as quickly as they came.

She had a rack of CDs filled and was halfway through a second when he returned.

"This is a treat, let me tell you," he said with a smile as he began to unload the bag he carried. Shifting a carton from the low coffee table onto the floor, he spread out not only lobster rolls, but cups of potato salad, ears of corn and soda. "Take-out for me is usually McDonald's."

Instinctively Nina knew that the choice had nothing to do with money. "That's what your son likes?"

"He *loves* it. He'd be happy to go there every day of the week if I let him."

"What does he eat?"

"A hamburger, a small bag of fries and a milk shake. He doesn't always make it through the shake, but he devours the rest. For a little guy, he always amazes me."

"He's four?"

John nodded. Sitting down on a nearby carton, stretching his legs comfortably before him, he took a bite of a lobster roll, closed his eyes, chewed softly and neatly. "Mmm," he said with feeling, "is this good."

Nina, too, took a carton as a seat. Using one of the plastic forks that had tumbled from the bag, she sampled the potato salad. "So's this." She took another bite, all the while thinking about her curiosity and the fact that maybe, now that she and John were friends, she could ease it. It seemed she'd been wondering about certain things for a long time.

Shooting for nonchalance, she took a sip of soda, then said, "Tell me about your son."

John's glasses might have hidden the flash of wariness in his eyes had she not been watching him closely. Clearly he guarded his son. She wondered if he'd tell her to mind her own business—one part of her was telling herself that very same thing—and felt deeply warmed when, instead, he said in a low, slow voice, "J.J.'s a sweet little boy who's had a rough go of it in life."

"When did his mom die?"

"When he was one. He doesn't remember her."

"Is that good or bad?"

"Good, I guess. He doesn't know what he's missing."

Nina wanted to ask how the woman had died, but didn't. It was enough that John had agreed to talk about his son. "I'm sure you give him twice the love."

"I try," he said thoughtfully, and took another mouthful of lobster roll. After he'd swallowed, he said, "It's hard sometimes knowing if what I'm doing is right. Normal guidelines don't fit when it comes to J.J. He's a special child."

Eating her own lobster roll, she waited for him to go on. As curious as she was, she didn't want to sound nosy. Surprisingly the silence wasn't awkward. She ate patiently, wondering about all those ways in which J.J. might be special.

Finally John raised his eyes to hers. "What have you heard about him?"

"Just that he has vision and hearing deficiencies."

"That's pretty much it. He wears glasses and hearing aids." With the words, John looked momentarily in pain. "God, it hurts to see him sometimes. My heart aches for the poor little kid. He didn't ask for any of this."

"What caused it?"

He thought about that for a minute, then shrugged. "No one knows. He was born that way."

"Did you know right then?"

He shook his head. "Things seemed fine at the beginning. By the time he was six months old, I could tell that he wasn't responding to sound. It was when I brought him in to be tested that they detected the problem with his eyes. Unfortunately, there wasn't much of a medical nature that they could do about either. They wouldn't even fit him for glasses until he was close to a year. He'd have just dragged them off."

"They must help."

He nodded. "A lot. He reads."

"At four?"

John shot her a quintessentially parent-proud grin. "Nothing's wrong with his mind. He's a bright little kid."

"I'm sure," Nina said.

"I wasn't. Given all the other problems, I'd been told there was a possibility that he'd be retarded. Thank goodness that isn't so. I mean, how much should the child have to take?"

"But you'll be putting him in a special school." That was what she'd been told, the major reason John had invested in Crosslyn Rise. Handled wisely over the years, the profit he stood to make would cover the high cost of that special school.

"I have to. What hearing he has is negligible. He has to learn how to sign, how to read lips and how to talk."

"That'll all start next year?"

"It all started as soon as we diagnosed the problem. He and I work with a therapist every morning, and in the afternoon he's in a play group with children like him. Their parents are trained like I am. The learning for these kids has to be continuous." His eyes widened and he shot a hurried glance at his watch. The abrupt movement, coming from him, took Nina by surprise. Seeing the time, he let out a breath. "I'm okay. He's with one of those other families today, but I still have a few minutes."

"Oh, John, I feel guilty. It can't be often that you get a free afternoon like this, and to blow it away unpacking my things. I'm really sorry."

He regarded her strangely. "Don't be. If I hadn't wanted to do this, I wouldn't have. You didn't exactly invite me." He paused. "You didn't exactly *want* me. I inflicted myself on you, so you don't have anything to feel guilty about." He paused again. "Besides, I got a lobster roll out of it. And some interesting conversation." His voice lowered. "I like you better when you're talking books than when you're talking real estate."

"The feeling's mutual," Nina said, then regretted it the moment the words were out because, behind his glasses, John's eyes darkened. "You're not as bad as I thought you'd be," she added quickly, lest he think she was being suggestive in any way, shape or form.

His eyes remained dark. They dropped to her mouth.

"I think," she babbled on, "that when you only see a person in one context, say for matters involving a business deal like Crosslyn Rise, you get a very narrow view." Her voice seemed to be fading, like the rest of her was doing. Fading, weakening, feeling all warm and trembly inside. "It's nice to know you like lobster rolls."

John's brows drew together in a brief frown before he managed to drag his eyes back to hers. "I do," he said quietly. "But I'd better go, I think." He stood.

Simply so that she wouldn't feel so overwhelmed, Nina stood, too. "Thanks." She waved a hand in the vague direction of the food, then broadened the gesture. "For everything."

He walked slowly to the door, one hand deep in his pocket reaching for his keys, his head slightly bent.

Nina was suddenly nervous. "John? I didn't upset you, asking about your son, did I?"

"No, no." He pulled the keys from his pocket, but he didn't turn.

She moved closer. "I was curious. That's all."

They keys jangled in his hands. "People are."

She moved closer still. "You must be a very good parent. I'm beginning to feel a little humbled."

"That makes two of us."

She frowned. "Two?"

Slowly he turned, and what she saw in his eyes took her breath away. His voice was low, still slow but nowhere near as smooth as it usually was. "I thought I was immune to women like you. I thought that there was no way a woman with a fast-driving career could turn me on, but I was wrong."

A tiny voice inside Nina told her she ought to be angry, to either lash back or turn in the opposite direction and run, but that voice was drowned out by the sound of her pulse beating rapidly, hammering her feet in place on the floor.

His hand shaped her cheek, then slid along her jaw until his fingers were feathered by her hair. "Tell me not to want to kiss you," he said.

But she couldn't. As outlandish as it seemed, given that John Sawyer was the antithesis of the kind of man she usually liked, she wanted his kiss. Maybe, deep down inside, she'd been wanting it since he'd shown up at her door that afternoon wearing a T-shirt that made his chest look heart-stoppingly hard and broad. Maybe she'd been wanting it even longer, since the night she'd shown up at his store and seen him sweating. There was something about sweat that blew the intellectual image. Sweat was earthy and honest. Sweat was intimate. Given the right chemistry between a man and a woman, it was a powerful aphrodisiac.

Whether she wanted it to be so or not, Nina had to accept that the chemistry between John and her was right. There was no way her body was letting her move away from his touch, no way it was letting her evade him when his head slowly lowered and his mouth touched hers.

He gave her one kiss, then a second, then a third. Each one lasted a little longer than the one before, each one touched her a little more deeply. He seemed to be savoring her, reluctantly, if his words were to be considered, but savoring her nonetheless. His lips were firm, knowing, increasingly open and wet. His kisses were smooth as warm butter and ten times more hot.

By the time the last one ended and he raised his head, Nina's breath was coming in short, shallow wisps. Her eyes were closed. She felt miles and miles away from everything she'd always known, transported to a place where kisses touched the heart. She'd never been there before.

"I shouldn't have done that," he said quietly.

She opened her eyes to find his face flushed, his eyes serious. "Probably not," she said softly.

"You're not my type."

"Nor you mine."

"So why did it happen?"

She tried to think up an eloquent answer, but for all the hard selling she'd done in her day, she was without one. The best she could do was to murmur, "Chemistry?"

After a minute's thought, he said, "I guess." As though the admission were a warning, he passed his thumb over her lips—moist now, warm and naturally rouged—before letting his hand fall to his side.

"I didn't come here for this," he said gruffly. "I hope you know that."

She did. Somehow, with John, it wouldn't have occurred to her otherwise. He wasn't a wily sort of man.

"I'm not looking for anything," he went on, still in that same gruff voice. "I don't have time for this kind of thing. Between the store and my son, I have all I can handle."

"Hey," she said, taking a step back, "I'm not asking for anything." It sounded to her as though he thought she was, or would. "It wasn't *me* who started that kiss."

"You didn't tell me to stop."

"Because I was curious about it. But it's no big thing. It's over and done. Curiosity satisfied. Period."

He thought about that, then nodded. But he didn't turn to leave. Instead, he looked thoughtful again. Then, in a low voice, he said, "Was it good?"

She took a deep breath. "You don't really want to know."

"I want to know."

"It won't help the situation."

"I want to know."

"It'll only make you angry, because the last thing you want is for someone like me to say it was good."

"Was it?"

"John," she pleaded, "why don't you just leave it be?"

"Because I want to know," he said with the stubbornness of a child. Nina had the sudden fear that he would stand there asking until she told him the truth.

Staring him in the eye, she said, "Yes, it was good. It was very good, and I'm sorry it ended. But it had to, because it wasn't right. We're totally different people with totally different wants and needs. You can't understand why I talk so fast, and I can't understand why you talk so slow. I want to make money, you want to meditate on the beach." Her hands went in opposite directions. "Worlds apart, John, we're worlds apart."

"Yeah." His amber eyes moved over her features. "It's too bad. You're awful cute."

She snorted. "Cute is what every woman over thirty wants to be."

"Over thirty?"

"Thirty-one, to be exact."

His mouth quirked at the corner. "I wouldn't have guessed it."

That quirking annoyed her. She didn't like being laughed at. "Well, now you know, and since you do, you can understand that I mean all I say about what I'm doing and where I'm going. I'm not some cute little pixie fresh out of college trying to make it big. I've had years of training in my field, and now that I'm on the verge of getting where I want to be, I'm not letting anyone stand in my way." She stole in a breath and raced on. "So if you think that I'm going to think twice about that kiss, that I'm going to look for a replay or want something *more*, you're mistaken. I'm off and running, and you'll only slow me down. I won't let that happen."

Having said her piece in a way that she felt was forceful and clear, she stood her ground with her jaw set, waiting for John to do his thinking thing then come up with a rejoinder. Not more than thirty seconds had passed, though, when, with a start, he glanced at his watch.

"Damn," he muttered, "I'm late." Raising his arm in a wave, he was fast out the door, taking the stairs at a speedy trot. Nina had never seen him move so fast, but it made sense that if he did it for anyone, he would do it for his son, and she was glad. From what he said, the boy had precious little going for him but a good brain and a loving dad.

Standing there amid the cartons in the living room that didn't feel quite hers yet, Nina's mind traveled back in time to when she'd been four herself. She hadn't had any obvious handicap. Her vision had been fine, along with her hearing, and her mind had been sharp—too sharp, in some respects. Even at that age she had wondered why she didn't have a father. Even then she had known something was wrong when she'd heard gruff voices coming from her mother's room late at night. Even then she had known that the bruises on her mother's face and arms and legs weren't normal.

She sighed. Ignorance would have been bliss back then, but what was done was done. She'd overcome those things that had darkened her early years and was now well on her way to having the security she wanted. Okay, so once in a while she wished things were different. Once in a while she wished *she* had someone rush home to her the way John Sawyer had to his son. But life wasn't perfect, she knew. No one had everything. So if she didn't have that special someone who cared, she had a growing career and a growing name and lots of respect along the way. She could live with that. She had no other choice.

COME EIGHT O'CLOCK that night, she wasn't thinking of choices. Having unpacked the very last carton, the only thing on her mind was soaking in a hot, hot bath. Stripping out of her shirt and jeans, she started the water and returned to the bedroom for a robe, when the phone rang.

Absurdly, her first thought was that the phone would also be ringing at her old apartment, jangling through rooms now empty and forlorn. Remembering the good two years she'd had there, she felt a twinge of sadness.

Her second thought was that Lee was calling in to report on any activity that had taken place at the office that day. Shrugging into the robe, she reached for the phone.

"Hello?"

"Nina?"

It was a man's voice. Though she hadn't ever heard it before on the phone, she knew instantly whose it was. Thoughts of him had been hovering at the back of her mind since he'd left her house in such a rush.

"Hi," she said cautiously.

"It's John."

"I know."

The line was silent for a time before he said, "I, uh, just wanted to apologize for leaving so abruptly. Time had gotten away from me and J.J. was due home."

"Did you get back in time?"

"Almost."

"No?"

"They were waiting out front in the car."

"For long?"

"Three or four minutes. I'm usually on time. They were starting to worry."

"How about J.J.?"

"He was okay."

"Did he have fun?"

"I think so. Sometimes it's hard to tell whether he had a good time or he's just real happy to be home. One thing's for sure. He ate enough. He was wearing mustard, fruit punch and chocolate all over his shirt."

"Oh, yuck." She thought about single parenthood, and a sudden fear struck. "Are you the one who has to do the wash?"

"You got it."

"Oh, *yuck.*"

"Actually, given all I've had to clean up in the last four years, the dribbles from a picnic lunch are a snap."

Nina found herself picturing those other things. "You changed diapers?"

"All the time."

"What a good father. And husband. Your wife must have appreciated that." Once the words were out, she held her breath.

"Actually," he said after a brief pause, "she took it pretty much for granted. It was part of the bargain we made. I wanted the baby. She agreed to carry it if I was willing to take the responsibility for its care once it was born."

"That's awful," Nina exclaimed without thinking, then she did think and regretted the outburst. If John had adored his now-dead wife, the last thing Nina wanted to do was criticize her. "I mean, I suppose people do what's right for them. Did it work for her?"

"Not particularly. She went right back to work the way she planned, but she felt guilty, and she resented that."

"Oh, dear."

"Yeah." He paused. "Well." Another pause, then a new breath. "Anyway, I'm used to doing everything for J.J. It's kind of fun. Gives me a real sense of self-sufficiency."

Nina thought about that. "Do you cook?"

"Nothing gourmet, but he doesn't mind that. He's big on things like BLTs, and PB and Fs."

"PB and Fs?"

"Peanut butter and fluff sandwiches. Not quite the kind of meal you make, I'm sure."

Remembering the exchange they'd had over cookbooks in his store, Nina felt sheepish. "I don't really do that much."

"Ha," he scoffed. "I'm the one who unpacked your kitchen today. I saw that wok and that clay pot and that fondue dish."

"Those are all for fun. I don't use them often, except maybe for the wok. When I want a quick meal and don't feel like a frozen dinner, I stir-fry something up. I'm pretty good at it, actually. I've found some good recipes. I'll make you something sometime, if you'd like."

For the third time in the conversation, words had slipped from her mouth that she hadn't consciously put there. The idea that John Sawyer, whom she worked with but with whom she didn't have another thing in common except a love for reading, should want to come back to her house—for dinner, no less—was ridiculous. Surely he'd see that.

"Yeah," he said, "well, maybe." He paused. "So. Did you finish with the rest of your things?"

Feeling as though she'd been eased from a precarious place, she said, "Sure did. I'm feeling it now."

"Sore?"

"Mmm. I was just about to get in the—oh, hell! Hold on! I forgot about the water!" All but dropping the phone on the floor, she raced into the bathroom in time to watch the first of a steaming waterfall cascade over the edge of the tub. Frantically twisting the taps, she turned off the water, pulled out the plug, then reached for the towels she'd so recently hung on the nearby bar. "Good show, Nina," she muttered to herself as she mopped up the spillage. When she had the worst of it absorbed, she dropped the sodden towels into the sink, replaced the plug with just enough water left for her bath and returned to the phone.

"I can't believe I did that," she said without prelude. "A fine thing it'd be if the first night I'm here, I send water dripping onto my landlord's head."

"All cleaned up?"

"Enough." Thinking of the still-damp floor, she sighed. "I'd better go finish. Thanks for calling, John. And thanks again for your help. It was nice."

Some time later, lying in the tub with the heat of the water seeping into her tired limbs, Nina realized that it had been nice, both his help and his call. He was a nice man. A *sexy* man. All wrong for her, of course, and there was no point in even *thinking* of a repeat of that kiss. Still, he was nice to be with—which was what she told Lee the next morning when she was asked about the car that had been parked behind her car that Sunday afternoon.

"I was going to stop in and see how you were doing," Lee explained, "but when I saw that, I figured you already had a guest. I never thought it'd be John Sawyer." Her eyes narrowed in play. "Is there something you haven't told me?"

"Nothing at all," Nina said, cool and composed from the top of her shiny black hair to the toes of her shiny purple shoes. "John Sawyer is someone I work with. He knew I was moving, so he stopped by to help."

"I thought he drove you nuts."

"He does when it comes to work. But he's good for lifting cartons. So I used him." More pointedly she said, "That's what you have to learn to do. Turn the tables on Tom. Use him for a change, rather than the other way around."

"I'm not moving."

"Then use him for something else. Ask him to bring the wine and dessert if you're the one who's cooking dinner. Ask him to give you a lift to the service station when you have to pick up your car."

Lee wrinkled her nose. "I don't think he'd appreciate that."

"Probably not." Her voice gentled. "He does things on his terms, and his terms alone. That's not good. It's not fair."

Lee shrugged. "Maybe not, but that's the way it is."

Not for me, Nina thought. *Never for me.* She had her work. It, and the reward it brought, were all she needed.

With that reminder, she swiveled around to face her computer, punched up the current listings and got busy.

5

OUT OF SIGHT was not out of mind. Nina tried not to think about John. She tried not to think about the way he looked or the way he acted. Mostly she tried not to think about the way he kissed, but it didn't work. Memory was insidious, wending through her mind in brief but potent flashes.

She hadn't had a kiss like that since...she'd *never* had a kiss like that. In her experience, men kissed women either rapaciously, showing their hunger and proud of it, or timidly, showing their fear, hoping to pass it off as sensitivity. John hadn't kissed her either of those ways. His kiss had been forceful in a quiet, thoughtful way, which was pretty much how he was himself. He'd known what he was doing. His mouth had conveyed the attraction he felt. The fact that the attraction was unbidden made it all the more special.

But it was over, and she had put it from her mind, so she immersed herself in her work for all she was worth. It wasn't hard, since she loved what she did. And there was plenty to keep her busy. If she wasn't out showing a piece of property, she was working with the newspaper on fresh copy or doing paperwork for an impending sale or tracking down a competitor with a co-broke offer. When she was in the office, her phone was forever ringing.

None of those calls were from John. As the week wore on, during those brief in-between times when she thought of him, she began to wonder why he hadn't called. He had been so persistent at first that they discuss Crosslyn Rise, and though the decision on pricing had been made, the consortium had very clearly asked them to continue to work together.

She wondered whether he was as bothered, after the fact, by that kiss as she was.

She wondered whether he was embarrassed. Or disappointed. Or disgusted.

She wondered whether he hated her.

By Friday afternoon, she'd just about had it with the wondering. Picking up the phone, she punched out his number.

He answered, his voice deep and pleasantly resonant. "The Leaf Turner."

"John? It's Nina. Am I getting you at a bad time?" Heart pounding, she waited.

His voice came back a little less deep than it had been. "No, not at all. There's actually a comfortable lull here right now. How are you?"

She chose to believe he was pleased that she'd called. "Fine," she answered lightheartedly. "And you?"

"Can't complain."

"How's J.J.?" she asked, knowing it was the one thing that would guarantee a positive response.

"Great. The girls took him out for ice cream. He loves that."

"Girls, plural?"

"Two. Twins. What with J.J.'s problems, I like knowing there are two of them, so that one can keep an eye on him at any given time. You know how baby-sitters can be."

Actually she didn't. An only child herself, she'd never had a baby-sitter, but had been left with a neighbor or, at a frighteningly tender age, alone. Her mother hadn't had the money to pay a sitter. By virtue of that same fact, when Nina had been old enough to work, she had bypassed baby-sitting in favor of a supermarket job with more regular hours and higher pay. It hadn't mattered that the supermarket didn't hire kids under fifteen. She had talked them into hiring her. Even back then, she'd had a persuasive mouth.

"Do they talk on the phone a lot?" she asked.

"It's not as much that, as getting distracted cooking pizza or watching television. Actually, these two are pretty responsible. And they think J.J. is adorable."

"I'll bet he is," Nina said, because if he looked anything like John, she was sure he was. "Did you get all the mustard and stuff out?"

"The what? Oh, that. Pretty much."

Again she pictured him doing the wash and felt admiration. He was a good father. A good man.

Aware of the silence, she cleared her throat and said, "Uh, I'm actually calling about work, John. I picked up the finished brochures from the printer today. They're the ones we'll be handing out at the open house, and then, after that, in the office to anyone interested in Crosslyn Rise. I thought you might like to see them."

"That would be nice," he said with what she could have sworn was a touch of caution.

"I'll be working most of the weekend, so I'll be in and out, but I have to man the front desk at the office Sunday morning from ten to twelve." She had thought it all out. Her calling him was a business move. She didn't want him thinking it was anything else. Hence, the office. "Do you want to stop by then?"

After a pause, he said, "I could do that."

"You could bring J.J. if you want." He certainly didn't have to hire a sitter for something as innocent as a brief office meeting. "We won't be long. You'll probably want to take the brochure home to study. I'll be passing out copies to all of the members of the consortium at our next meeting, but I thought you might want to see it before then. There may be some things that you think are stronger or weaker, that we can compensate for in person at the open house."

"Okay. I'll drop by."

"Sometime between ten and twelve?"

"Uh-huh."

She shrugged. That was that. "See you then."

SHE TOLD HERSELF that it was nothing more than another business meeting and probably wouldn't last longer than two minutes, still she took care in dressing, again passing over some of the more outlandish of her outfits in favor of a relatively sedate slacks set. Granted, the pants were harem-style and the top short and loose, but the color was moss green, the neck barely scooped and the sleeves as voluminous as the legs.

Well, hell, he didn't expect that she'd dress like a schoolmarm, did he? At least, the outfit wasn't neon pink, like some of hers were, and her nails weren't red now, but beige.

Ten o'clock came and went. She talked with a couple who walked in off the street, people who thought *maybe* they'd look for something new but *only* if they could sell their old place and what were their chances of that? Ten-fifteen became ten-thirty. One of Martin's clients came by to drop some papers he'd signed. A potential buyer called to check on the time of another open house. Ten forty-five passed and eleven arrived.

She was beginning to wonder whether he'd forgotten, when, shortly before eleven-thirty, he came leisurely through the door. He was alone; she felt an unexpected stab of disappointment at that. But the disappointment was brief, because he looked so good. His hair was damp, freshly combed back over his ears and down over his nape. He was wearing a white shirt—open at the neck, with the sleeves rolled—and a pair of jeans that looked relatively new. She wondered if it was his Sunday best.

When he planted himself directly before her desk, she smiled. "You've been at the beach again." His skin had a golden glow, a bit of new color over what she'd seen the week before.

He nodded. "This morning. J.J. is still there."

Her face dropped. "Oh, I'm sorry, John. I didn't mean to drag you away from him. This wasn't so important. We could have done it another time."

"You didn't drag me away. He's with friends. He's happy."

"The same friends who took him out last week?"

He shook his head. "Different ones. They have a daughter with special needs. She's just about J.J.'s age. They're in the same play group."

"Do all the children in the play group have similar handicaps?"

"Roughly."

"How many children?"

"Twelve."

She was stunned. "And they all live around here?" She couldn't imagine so many four-year-olds with similar problems in the immediate area. As populations went, the local tally was low.

"No. Some of them come from pretty far, which means that we go pretty far to see them in return. But it's worth it. Socialization is critical, but it's hard for kids like these to get it through regular channels. I tried J.J. in a local play group when he was two. I figured that he was doing all the same things the other kids were, playing with blocks and all. But he wasn't talking. Since he couldn't hear, he couldn't react to the other kids the way they expected. And he made the mothers nervous."

Nina thought that was awful. "Screw *them*."

He gave a lopsided grin that created a dimple in his cheek—and sent a ripple of awareness through Nina. "I felt the same way. Actually, I felt worse. I was furious. Then I thought about it, and I talked it over with J.J.'s therapists, and the way we reasoned it out, it wasn't so awful. Those women were nervous because they didn't know how to communicate with J.J. They kept expecting him to be just like their own kids, only he wasn't. Isn't. And it didn't matter how angry I got, no way was that experience going to be positive, and that's the name of the game. So now he's with people who understand him. They understand me. We've all been through the same things. We help each other."

"Like watching kids at the beach?"

"Like that."

Nina reached for the brochure that she'd tucked safely to the side. "You'll probably want to take this and leave, then." She held it out, trying to be a good sport. "It's a beautiful day for the beach. You'll be anxious to get back."

He closed his hand around it, but rather than turning away, he arched a questioning brow toward the chair by the desk. She was surprised, and delighted. With an enthusiastic, "Please," she watched him lower himself into the chair, stretch out his legs and open the brochure.

He really *was* handsome, she decided again. He wasn't urbane or sophisticated looking, certainly not slick, still he was handsome. Today there was something western about him. With his fresh jeans and his damp hair and the color the sun had painted on his skin, he looked like a cowboy newly off the range and showered. With high-heeled boots, the picture would have been complete. Then again, she preferred his deck shoes, particularly the way he wore them without socks. She wondered what his ankles were like, whether they were as well formed as his hands and wrists, and half wished he'd cross one of his legs so she could see.

But he didn't. Looking perfectly comfortable as he was, he took his time reading the copy, studying the drawings, closing the brochure to look at the piece as a whole. "This is very professional," he said at last.

She felt inordinately pleased. "Thank you. Do you think it'll impress the people we want to impress?"

"It should." He turned to the last page, where the price guides were listed. "I was wondering whether they'd get these right."

"You mean, you were wondering whether I'd hike those prices back up between the time the consortium voted and the printer printed?" She couldn't quite tell if he was kidding. Rather than overreact if he was, she kept her voice light. "I wouldn't do that, John."

He shrugged. "You never can tell with typos."

"There aren't any typos in that brochure. Not a single one. I've been over it with a fine-tooth comb dozens of times. It's perfect."

Taking several more minutes, he looked through it again. Then, unfolding himself from the chair, he stood. "I like it, Nina."

She hated to see him leave so soon. "I thought maybe you'd have some suggestions."

"This is pretty much a *fait accompli*, isn't it?"

"Yes, it's all printed, but that doesn't mean we can't approach things differently when we're talking with clients, if you think a different approach is called for." She was feeling a little foolish, because he was right. The brochure was done and printed. Everything major was correct. To change something small and reprint hundreds of copies would be an absurd expense.

Still, the consortium wanted them to work together.

Eyes on the brochure, he said, "Why don't I take this home and read it again—" his voice dropped and slowed "—when I'm not so distracted by the piles of soft stuff you're wearing." With each of the last words, his eyes rose a notch until finally they met hers. "I'll call you if anything comes to mind."

She swallowed. "That sounds okay."

He nodded. Raising two fingers in a wave that could have been negligent, bashful or reluctant, he left.

NINA MADE A POINT not to wait for his call. She figured that after the way she'd invited him over when she could as well have put the brochure in the mail, a little aloofness was called for. So she ran around as usual, confident that if he called the office, she'd get his message, and that if he called her at home, he'd keep calling until she was there.

It wasn't until Thursday night that she picked up her phone in response to its ring and heard his voice. "I still think the brochure is fine," he said after the briefest of exchanged hellos. "But I thought maybe we could go up to the Rise and take a look around. I haven't been there in a while. If you're looking for the reaction of an everyday Joe, I'm your man."

Not even at the beginning, when Nina had broken into cold sweats over John's pokey ways, had she thought of him as an everyday Joe, and she certainly didn't now. He was different. He marched to his own drummer. She did concede, though, that of all the consortium members, he was probably the one to give the most off-the-cuff response, so she supposed in a way he was right.

"Okay. When can you go?"

"Tomorrow morning, actually, but I know this is pretty last-minute for you. You probably have appointments all over the place."

She did. She didn't have to dig out her appointment book to know that, and when she did open it, she saw that her schedule was even worse than she'd thought. But John was free, and he was right. They really should get up to see Crosslyn Rise.

"I may be able to shift things around," she said, her mind already at work. "Can you give me half an hour to find out?"

"Sure. I'll call back."

During the next thirty minutes, Nina phoned four clients, one other broker and Lee. By the time John called back, she had cleared a two-hour stretch starting at ten. They agreed to meet then.

No matter how frequent a visitor Nina was to the Rise, she was always amazed at the progress she found with each return. Most impressive this time was the mansion. It had long since been scooped clean of its innards, with little left but structural elements such as the grand staircase and period details like ceiling moldings and chair rails. Renovation was well under way. Woodwork that had been stripped and sanded was now being stained. Walls were being modified, doorways shifted from one spot to another. From the large first-floor room that would serve as an elegant paneled meeting-room-lounge-library, to the large back room that would be a health club, to the totally modernized kitchen, the two private dining rooms, and the charming suites on the second floor that could be rented out to guests, the place was suddenly taking on the feel of something on the verge of being real.

"Does this ever look different," John said as he stood with his head tipped back to take in the height of the huge front hall. "Very nice."

He wasn't bubbly. His voice was as quiet as ever. But Nina, who had studied his face closely in the recent past, could read the subdued excitement there. Taking excitement from that, she waved him on. "Come." She led him from one room to the next, pausing in the middle of each, letting the feel of the place seep in. At spots where there was active construction going on, they had to watch where they stepped and moved, and at those times, John either went first and took her arm to guide her by or cautioned her to take care.

Nina had never been one to cling to a man, but John's touch felt good. Particularly on bare skin. In deference to the June warmth, she had worn a sundress. It was bright yellow, actually little more than a long tank top that, once hiked up at the waist by a wide leather belt, grazed the top of her knees. She had also worn flats for the sake of walking, and the overall effect was to make her feel that much more delicate next to John, who, wearing jeans and an open-necked shirt—a horizontally striped one this time—looked surprisingly rugged.

She stayed close, under the guise of safety, until they reached the outdoors and the danger of flying wood chips was gone. She would have given him more room then, but he didn't move away. He stayed close by her side during the walk down the path toward the duck pond, where the first of the near-completed condos were.

"Such a gorgeous place," he said. "I don't know how Jessica was ever able to give it up."

"She had to. She couldn't keep it as it was, and we couldn't find a single seller who could afford the whole thing. So rather than seeing it broken down by a developer who didn't care a whit about the glory of the Rise, she decided to form the consortium and be the one to call the shots."

"Does she call them, or does Carter?"

Nina looked up to find a mischievous smile touching his mouth. Her gaze lingered on his mouth for a minute before she said, "Jessica does. Carter gives her input, and he runs the meetings, but in the end the decision is hers." She returned her eyes to the path.

"They seem happy."

"They are."

"I think she's pregnant."

Nina's eyes flew back to his. This time John seemed totally serious. "How do you know?"

"She has that look."

"You mean, radiance? For heaven's sake, John, that's a crock."

"It is not."

"When a woman is pregnant, she feels sick. Then fat and clunky. There's nothing radiant about being that way."

"Fine for you to say," John said, kicking aside a fallen twig. "You've never been pregnant. You don't know what the feeling's like."

She laughed. "And you do? I hate to tell you this, John—"

"I remember when my wife was pregnant," he said quietly. Coming to a stop, he looked off in the distance, seeing not the duck pond but another time years before. "She wasn't real happy about it, but I was. I thought it was a miracle, the idea of this little life growing inside her. Long before the baby moved, I could see the changes in her body. First her breasts, then her waist, nature doing its thing in a totally generic way. Maybe she was too close to be able to appreciate it. I was just that little bit removed, so I could see things in a broader scheme. Then, when I felt the baby move in her stomach, everything that had been so broad seemed to focus in on the fact that it was my child growing there." His breath caught on the intake. Seeming surprised by his own words, he looked quickly at Nina. "Sorry. I get carried away. It was an incredible experience."

Standing still beside him, she felt goose bumps running up and down her arms. "You make it sound incredible." And she could almost believe in radiance, because she could have sworn that was the look she had seen on John's face for the few seconds before he'd caught himself.

The look she saw now was more earthy, and there was no way his glasses could mask it. His eyes were on her goose bumps. "Cold?"

"No."

Lightly, starting at her wrists, he ran his hands up her arms. They stopped just shy of her shoulders to gently knead her skin. He watched their progress, first one, then the next. "It's too bad you don't want to have kids. You'd make a pretty mother."

Her skin felt hot where he touched it, and the heat was stealing inside. "People would have trouble telling me from the kids," she managed to say, though her voice was meager.

"Pregnant, I mean. You'd be pretty pregnant."

Her heart was racing. "Maybe more substantial."

"No." His eyes touched her breasts, which rose with each shallow breath she took. "You're substantial now. But it's different when you're pregnant. Not just added weight. Something else." His eyes slipped to her stomach, caressing it through the thin jersey material, causing the same kneading sensation that was so seductive on her arms. She could barely move, barely breathe. Slowly, searing a path along the way, his gaze rose and locked with hers. "I keep thinking about you, Nina. I don't want to, but I do."

At the reluctant admission, she started to shake her head, but he made a shushing motion with his mouth and that stopped her. His voice was low, slow and sandy. "I keep remembering that kiss. It was so good. The only problem was that nothing touched but our mouths."

"I know," she whispered.

While his hands kept up their gentle motion, his thumbs slid sensuously up and down under the thin straps at her shoulders. "I keep wondering what it would be like to touch other places. I lie in bed at night imagining. It's not fun."

She swallowed. "Because you don't want to like me?"

"Because I get hard."

Her breath caught in her throat and stayed there despite the wild skittering of her pulse. She gave a short, sharp shake of her head.

"What?"

"Don't say things like that," she begged.

"Because it embarrasses you?"

"Because it excites me."

The flare in John's eyes told her what her words had done. His thumbs began moving more widely, stroking her skin in small patches that inched downward, under the edge of her dress, over the starting swell of her breast.

"I want to touch you more," he said. With the lightest pressure, he brought her arms just that tiny bit forward to angle her body better for his seeking thumbs. They stroked deeper, even deeper, under her bra now, moving toward the center of her breasts.

Her nipples tightened. "John," she whispered weakly. Heat seemed to be gathering and pooling not only in her breasts, but down low. She clutched his hips for support.

"Let me," he whispered back, as his thumbs reached their twin goals. He circled them once, touched their tips, then moved back and forth in a gentle rubbing.

Catching in a small cry, Nina bit her lip. But the feeling in her breasts was still too intense, so she closed her eyes and dropped her head back.

With a low groan, John caught her to him. His hands left her breasts and circled her, drawing her fully into his body at the same time that his mouth came down on hers. He kissed her long and deep, first with his lips, then his tongue. Wrapping her arms around his neck, she sought his firmness. Opening her mouth wide to his, she tasted his hunger. There was nothing in him that was either rapacious or arrogant. He kissed her like a man who simply needed to be closer.

And closer he brought her. His arms swept over her back, one lower, one higher, pressing her into him at every point. His strength came at her through his thighs, his chest, his arms, made all the more enticing to her by the faint tremor that spoke of his restraint.

When he finally tore his mouth away, his breathing was ragged. Dragging his arms from around her, he took her face in his hands. "What the hell am I going to do with you?"

She didn't know what to say.

"Can you feel how much I want you?"

She hadn't been that long without a man that she didn't know the meaning of the hard presence against her stomach. Unable to take her eyes from his, she nodded.

"So?" he asked in frustration.

"So I don't sleep around."

"Me, neither."

"I don't take making love lightly."

"Me, neither."

"So we can't do it. We're all wrong for each other. We don't even like each other. And we have to work together."

He looked at her for a long time, his amber eyes dark and hungry still. "You're right." His thumbs skimmed her cheeks. "But all that doesn't take the wanting away. I haven't wanted a woman—"

He was cut off by the intrusion of a loud voice on the approach. "Okay, you guys, I think you'd better break it up."

Nina's head shot around as quickly as John's, and she found herself staring into the amused eyes of Carter Malloy, who was coming from the direction of the duck pond. Stopping not far from them, he said, "I think there's something about the air out here. It makes you forget that just anyone could be walking through. Fortunately for you, it's me. I understand these things."

Nina knew her cheeks were red, but she didn't say a word either in defense of herself or protest to John when he slowly released her.

Carter scratched the back of his head. "I nearly lost it with Jessica, just about a year ago, not far from where you stand." He paused, looking from Nina's face to John's. "I think the ducks were less embarrassed then than you two are now."

Nina took a deep, faintly shuddering breath. "You should have called from way back on the path."

"I did."

"Oh."

John had his hands on his hips. "You should have called a second time."

"I did. But, hey, now that you're awake and aware, I'll just be moving along." He gave them a grin and started off. "Catch you later."

He'd gone a good ten yard when Nina called, "Carter, is Jessica pregnant?"

He stopped in his tracks and turned, wearing a guarded look. "Where did you hear that?"

"Is it true?"

Taking a deep breath that straightened his back and expanded his chest beneath the blazer and shirt he was wearing, Carter allowed himself a slow smile. "Yeah, it's true. She miscarried in January, so we've been cautious about saying anything. But she's almost into her fourth month. Things look good this time."

Forgetting her embarrassment, Nina burst into a grin. "Hey, that's great. I knew she wanted a baby."

"We both do."

"How's she feeling?" John asked.

Carter shimmied a hand. "Sometimes nauseous, sometimes not. The doctor says the sickness is a sign that the baby's really settling in, which is good news after the first one. We're keeping our fingers crossed."

"I'll keep mine crossed, too," Nina said.

John put a thumb up and said in a very male way, "Good goin', Carter."

Carter tossed him a macho smile before turning and continuing along the path.

Watching him go, Nina murmured under her breath, "Are you going to say, 'I told you so'?"

"Of course not. The important thing is that it's true."

"Mmm. She did tell me she wanted a baby. I'm excited for her."

"Excited about the baby?"

"Excited because she's getting what she wants. I don't know enough about babies to get excited about them."

"Don't have any friends with kids?"

"A few. But I've never been terribly involved. I'm too busy with work. My friends seem to know that. When they meet me for lunch, it's without the kids." She allowed herself a glance at John. "Which is another reason why you and I are no good. You have a kid. I wouldn't know what in the devil to do with one."

John didn't say anything. He stood there, looking down at her, looking *into* her, seemingly, for something she was sure wasn't there. Looking back at him, all she could see was the random brush of his hair on his brow, the lean contour of his jaw, the straight slash of his nose, the tightness of his lips. It was a face that drew her even when she told herself that it shouldn't.

Finally he raised his head and looked away. "We'd better get going."

Nodding, she started off toward the duck pond, but the glow that had earlier been on the day was gone. In its place was a tension that began in the body and ended in the mind, causing an awkwardness that was under-written with need.

They walked through the condominium that was to be the model, then through two others. Nina pointed out various features and options, just as she might have if John had been an interested buyer. They avoided looking at each other, avoided standing too close, but that didn't ease the wire that seemed strung taut be-tween them. Whatever the distance, it hummed.

By the time they returned to the mansion, Nina was feeling strung out, herself. She was only too glad to put together a hasty goodbye to John, climb into her car and drive off. She wasn't used to confusion. Hitherto in her life, she had been the sole master of her fate. Now, though, it seemed she was losing control, if not of her fate, then of *something*.

She wished she knew what that something was.

She wished she could stop it from slipping away.

She wished she didn't feel hot, then cold, light, then dark, good, then bad.

Mostly she wished she understood what she was feeling for John. He wasn't like any man she'd ever known. He was maddeningly laid-back, but she respected him. He saw the world differently from her, but she trusted him. She liked him, but she didn't.

And she wanted him. Wanted him. He haunted her for the rest of the day and all that night. She lay in bed wide awake, remembering how he'd kissed her and held her, how safe she'd felt, how valued, how hot and needy. The need returned, making her flop one way then the next, but no position was better for the aching within. *I lie in bed imagining,* he'd said, and she imagined him imagining. She also imagined him hard, and the fever built.

She slept for an hour, then awoke, slept for another, awoke again. When her skin grew damp in the warmth of the night, she sponged herself off, but no sooner did she return to bed than she was sweaty again.

By dawn, she was fit to be tied. No man, *no man,* she vowed, could do this to her. No man was worth it. She had her life, and it was free and independent, just as she wanted. Once she had her own agency, that independence would increase. She was well on her way to where she wanted to be. She didn't need any man, *any man.*

Then, at eight o'clock, her doorbell rang. Sticky, tired and more than a little cranky, she plodded down the stairs. "Who is it?" she yelled through the wood.

"John," he called back.

Moaning softly, she put her forehead to the worn pine. It was cool, with a faint musty scent that took her out of time and place, but the relief was short-lived. John was on the other side. She didn't know what to do.

His voice came more quietly, as though he'd moved closer. "Open the door, Nina. We need to talk."

"I don't think," she said, squeezing her eyes shut, "that this is the best time."

He didn't answer. Had he been another man, she might have wondered if he'd left. But this was John.

After a minute, he spoke again, still quiet, still close. "Nina? Open the door, Nina. Please?"

She might have had a comeback had it not been for his tone of voice. Not even the thickness of the door could muffle the quiet command. But there was something else there, something even more potent. Beneath the quiet command was a hint of pleading.

Fearing she was making a huge mistake but helpless to avoid it, she gave a tiny sound of frustration, took a small step back and opened the door a crack.

6

JOHN PUSHED THE DOOR open only enough to slip through. Watching him from the corner by the hinge, Nina felt beset by every one of the wild imaginings she'd tried to stifle through the night. The fact that he wore a T-shirt and shorts didn't help any. The sight of leanly muscled legs spattered with warm brown hair stirred the fire inside her to a greater head.

"I brought donuts," he said quietly, but his eyes hadn't risen above her neck.

She was in the short nightie that she'd put on in the wee hours, and wore nothing beneath it. "I was in bed," she said, feeling the need to explain. She wouldn't normally have answered the door dressed that way. But she felt reckless, at the end of her tether. "It was a bad night."

At that, he did raise his eyes. He'd left his glasses at home, and it struck her that he looked every bit as sweaty as she felt. His hair was damp and disheveled, his skin moist. "I ran." His eyes were intent, the deepest, richest amber she'd ever seen. "I thought we could talk."

"I don't know if I can." Her need was written all over her face, she knew, but she couldn't erase it.

John seemed to see it, consider it, fight it—with about as much success as she had. After an eternity of searing silence, he muttered, "I don't want these." Dropping the bag of donuts onto the stair, he reached for her.

Coming up against his body, winding her arms around his neck, feeling him lift her nearly off her feet, Nina felt the first relief she'd had in hours. She sighed his name and held tighter, burying her face against his neck.

For the longest time, they stood like that, holding each other tighter, then tighter still, making no sounds but those of quickened breathing and the occasional whimper or moan. Nina might have stayed that way forever if it wasn't for the gradual awakening of her body to the one molding it. She began to move against him in small ways to better feel him, and when that wasn't enough, she started to use her hands.

John's own hands made slow sweeps of discovery over her back. She could tell the instant he knew for sure she was bare under her nightie by the sharp catch of his breath. Fingers splayed, his hands stole up the back of her thighs to her bottom.

"Tell me to stop if you don't want this," he said in a gravelly voice she'd never heard before. It was laced with raw need and was a stimulant in itself.

"I want it," she breathed frantically. Exploring the lean line of his hips, she pushed her fingers over his thighs. The hair there abraded her palms delightfully. "I need it," she confessed just as frantically, then let out a cry when he touched the fire between her legs. "Help me," she begged, and to convince him, she worked her fingers up under his shorts. He wore cotton briefs, but they were stretched taut.

Clearly he didn't need any convincing.

Before she had any inkling of what he was doing, he slid his hands under her thighs and lifted her. When her legs were cinched around his hips, he covered her mouth with his and devoured it whole as he started up the stairs. He didn't stop until he was in her bedroom, where he lowered her to the rumpled sheets and crouched over her.

His voice a rough burr, he drew up her nightie. "I haven't been with anyone since my wife. Do I need a condom?"

Nina helped him pull the thin fabric over her head. As soon as one hand was freed, she reached for him. "It's been longer than that for me," she whispered hurriedly as she tugged at his shirt. It was over his head in an instant, revealing a chest that was well formed and tapering. A wide wedge of hair narrowed, arrowlike, toward his fly. She reached there and touched him. "No condom."

John lowered his zipper and shifted to thrust both shorts and briefs aside. "Babies?"

"I take pills," she gasped, then, "Hurry, John, hurry." His large hand swept her under him, and no sooner did she open her legs when, like a heat seeker, he was in. Stunned by the force of his impaling, she cried out and arched up.

"Nina—"

"No, no, it doesn't hurt, it feels good, so good."

But that penetration, that first feel of his masculine strength, was only the beginning. What he proceeded to do then nearly blew her mind. He stroked her inside and out, using his hands, his mouth, his sex. He nipped, he laved. He quickened the pace and the force when her breath came more quickly. At times his movements were rhythmic, at times less so. At times he filled her to the utmost, withdrew nearly all the way, then reentered with a sharp pulsing burst that she might have feared was climactic if he hadn't continued right on again.

Hungry for everything he gave her, she touched him wherever she could, but the heat he stoked in her soon drove everything from her mind except the release coming on. She erupted with a vengeance, throbbing against him for what seemed an eternity. Lost on the other side of rapture, she wasn't able to separate her climax from his until she finally returned to consciousness enough to feel the last of the spasms shaking his body.

Slowly, breathing hard, he lowered himself over her. After a long minute, he rolled to his side and drew her along, still inside her.

She looked into his eyes, and for a minute she couldn't speak. Something caught at her throat, something deep and emotional, something she couldn't—didn't want to—understand. Making love with John had been the experience of a lifetime.

As the minutes passed and she regained her poise, she let a smile soften her lip. "Who'd have guessed it?" she finally whispered.

His brow creased in a frown that was here and gone. "Guessed what?"

"That slow, quiet, thoughtful John Sawyer was a crackerjack of unleashed virility in bed."

His cheeks were already flushed, but she could have sworn they grew more so. "I was inspired."

"You certainly were." Her smile faded. She touched his face. "That was special."

He gave a slow, thoughtful nod. "Are you sure I didn't hurt you?"

"Do I look hurt?"

He shook his head. Slowly. "You look well loved." He touched her lips, which were still warm and swollen, then her cheek, then her hair. "How can hair that is shorter than mine be feminine?"

"It's not real hard to have hair shorter than yours," she quipped, and buried her fingers in the thickness at his nape, "but I like it."

"You didn't at first."

"I didn't like much about you at first. You were slowing me down."

"I still am. It's become my cause."

She assumed he was teasing and teased him right back. "It won't work."

"Sure, it will. You're not rushing off to work right now, are you?"

She shook her head. "I don't have to be in until ten."

"If you had to be in at nine, would you be rushing?"

"Maybe." She grinned. "I suppose it would depend on how forceful that *thing* you're anchoring me here with is. Doesn't feel too forceful right now."

He grinned back. "Give it a minute."

"You think so?"

"I know so."

She waited a minute, during which time she touched his chest, tracing the hair there, teasing his nipples. "Hmm," she said, clamping her thigh higher around his when she felt him growing inside her, "I think you may be right."

"Of course I'm right." He caught her mouth and ate at it gently, then less gently as his hunger grew. Fluidly he rolled to his back, bringing her up to straddle him. His eyes were focused on her breasts, which were warm and rose tipped. After guiding her hips for a deeper joining, he left her to her own devices there and touched her breasts.

Nina watched the long fingers she admired curved around her flesh. She watched them trace her shape and weigh her fullness. She watched them knead, then rub her nipples into hard beads, then draw her forward to meet his mouth. The sight of his tongue dabbing the tip of her breast with moisture that his finger then spread, was nearly her undoing. Closing her eyes, she began to move on him, shifting forward, then back and around, feeling him grow and grow inside her until he was rising to meet her thrusts.

He brought her to a first climax by tugging her nipples into elongated points. He brought her to a second one by finding the hard bud between her legs and stroking it to fruition. He brought her to a third one by rolling her over and plunging into her with the kind of savagery she'd never have expected from him, but which drove her wild. By the time he'd emptied himself into her, their bodies were slick and spent.

For a short time, they lay limp and quiet, and at first, Nina enjoyed the closeness. Then her mind clicked on. Slowly picking up speed, it ran her through what had happened, painting pictures of what it meant, and she grew frightened. She had enjoyed herself too much, far too much. John Sawyer as a lover could be habit-forming. But she didn't have room in her life for a relationship. She didn't have time for a man like John. She had places to go. She couldn't be tied down, *wouldn't* be tied down, not even by her own desires.

"Gotta get up," she murmured from against his chest.

His arm tightened around her. "No, stay."

"Gotta get to work."

"Call in. Get someone to cover."

"I can't."

"I have a sitter till noon."

A sitter. The word represented one of the major differences between Nina and John. Flattening a firm hand on his chest, Nina ignored the lure of damp, warmly furred male flesh and levered herself up. Seconds later, she was out of bed, headed for the bathroom.

"Nina?" John called.

"I have to shower," she called back.

"Put it off."

"I can't."

She turned on the water. As soon as steam rose from it, she stepped under and began to soap herself. She worked methodically, the same way she always did. If certain spots were more sensitive than usual, even tender, she ignored that. She went on to her hair, scrubbing it hard, then rinsed, turned off the water, reached for the towel and began to rub herself dry. By the time she returned to the bedroom, John was propped up against the brass headboard, looking extraordinarily masculine against her bright pink sheets. Everything in the room was bright pink for that matter; still he didn't look foolish. Just masculine.

Ignoring that, too, she took underwear from a drawer and put it on, then a pair of silk walking shorts and a matching silk blouse, both in fuchsia. After hooking a pair of turquoise spangles onto her ears, a matching necklace around her neck and a belt around her waist, she stepped into strappy sandals. Then she shook her head, vigorously, peered into the mirror over the dresser and finger-combed her hair.

"Nina."

She looked over at John in surprise. She hadn't forgotten he was there—no way could she do that—but